CW00495144

About the Author

Jo Jefferson is a former P.E. teacher, an experienced horsewoman and a former National Side Saddle Rider of the Year. She is a respected international Equestrian Judge having judged in Australia, New Zealand and South Africa. She has judged here in the UK at major County Shows, at The Horse of the Year Show and The Royal International Horse Show on numerous occasions. She is also to be found on the end of a microphone as an equestrian commentator at events up and down the country. Jo has a son and a daughter and lives in a cottage in the Yorkshire Dales.

A Horse's Tale

Jo Jefferson

A Horse's Tale

Olympia Publishers
London

www.olympiapublishers.com
OLYMPIA PAPERBACK EDITION

A CIP catalogue record for this title is
available from the British Library.

ISBN: 978-1-78830-281-4

First Published in 2019

Olympia Publishers
60 Cannon Street
London
EC4N 6NP

Printed in Great Britain

Dedication

To Tamzin and Sam

Acknowledgements

Wherever man has left his footprint in the long ascent from barbarism to civilization we will find the hoofprint of the horse beside it.

John Moore

Chapter One

The day when his life changed began pleasantly enough.

Jade, multi-pierced, black hair gelled and spiked into the frosty air, stomped across the yard. A bright bay face with a crooked white stripe looked expectantly over a stable door. He snorted loudly as he breathed in the crisp dawn air through flared nostrils and kicked out at the door, impatient for breakfast.

Humphrey was a handsome, well-bred, lightweight hunter. He knew that today was a hunting day because Jade, his groom, had plaited his mane last night and given him a late night feed. He stared across the valley at the rolling fields and the swathe of mist above the river, and shivered expectantly. Now seven years old, he had been hunting for two seasons. Following the laid scent trails, he carried his aged owner, Major Bentley, safely and well over post and rails, ditches and the impressive stone walls which formed such an integral part of the North Yorkshire countryside. He surveyed his world outside the loose box through wide, kind eyes which reflected a generous heart and giving nature. He had only known kindness in his seven years and found the world of men a pleasant and easy place in which to live.

He whinnied a greeting as Jade's familiar footsteps, those of muckers on gravel, scrunched towards him.

"Humphers old lad, how you doing?" Jade's cheerful greeting carried through the sharp winter air." I hope you haven't rubbed your plaits out, you little sod. Ready for breakfast, are we? Sorry, I'm a bit late but I went to the pub last night with Dan. I have a horrible headache from too many lagers. So don't you be banging about this morning. My head won't stand it!"

Throughout this speech Jade scratched the horse's ears affectionately and he nuzzled into her spiky thatch of raven black hair, still stiff from last night's over enthusiastic application of sculpture gel. Jade wore a very old but favourite black t-shirt emblazoned in gold with "Bollocks to Blair" on the back and "Silly Filly" on the front. The young man on the t-shirt stand at The Great Yorkshire Show years ago had told her it was a contradiction in terms but Jade replied that as people never read both together –what was the problem? The man had laughed, looked into the dark pools of her eyes and done the lettering free of charge.

At seventeen, Jade was a cheerful mixture of Punk and Goth with the most amazingly big, deep brown almost black, eyes. Admittedly they didn't quite look their brightest and best at this moment in time due to most of last night's mascara collecting in the corner and a tinge of red round the pupils. Jade also proved the saying that you can't judge a book by its cover because under the spiky hair, the eyebrow and tongue piercing, the row of studs in her left ear, the black lipstick and the tattoo of a snake just above her right shoulder blade, there beat a huge heart of gold.

You may be asking why this eclectic mix of style and character was working in Major Bentley's stable yard. The short answer is that his housekeeper was Jade's Aunt Dulcie. Despite initial reservations, the job was working well and both parties blessed the day two years ago when they had set age and cultural differences aside to 'see how it goes for a month's trial!'

Humphrey gave Jade a firm nudge on the S of Silly Filly just to say that he was hungry and would she please cut out the dawdling and hurry up with breakfast.

"Ouch! You horrible brute! OK! OK! Keep your hair on. I'm going right now." With that she gave his ear a final scratch and tramped across the yard to the feed store. Humphrey scowled and swished his tail as Jade made him wait until she'd emptied the feed into the manger.

"Manners maketh man *and* horse," she muttered as she stood back and Humphrey dived in, burying his nose, snorting and blowing his conditioning cubes and alfalfa mix all round the manger. Jade giggled. "Honestly you'd think you hadn't had anything to eat for years. Move over you great lump whilst I muck out." The horse moved over when asked and although he scowled and laid back his ears, Jade understood totally about feeling grumpy in a morning and she worked with quiet confidence disturbing him as little as possible. Once his feed was finished she groomed him thoroughly. Humphrey loved the feel of the soft brush on his skin and the soothing rhythm of her chatter.

"Now then 'H' you old rat bag," she chided. "You've bits of shavings all in your mane and tail and I haven't time to do your mane all over again. I should have found that old lycra hood and put that on to protect your plaits. Hindsight! It's such a wonderful thing! I'll just have to tidy it up the best I can. You can't go out hunting looking like a total scruffbag."

She picked out his hooves and H leant all his weight on her just because he felt like it and by the time she had finished, her mascara was looking even blotchier and her normally translucent pale skin had the same pink tinge as her eyes.

"Phew, that was hard work, you 'orrible 'orse. Right, rugs on, then I'm off in for breakfast." Jade gave Humphrey a parting tweak of the ears and stomped off towards the Manor House.

One hour later H was in his stable, tacked up, his travelling boots and rug on, waiting expectantly for his rider. However, it wasn't the slow, well-known footsteps of the Major he heard but a brisk unknown march across the gravel. Round the corner appeared a tall handsome young man, immaculately dressed in an expensive hunting coat, clinging breeches and 'poured into' riding boots, on the heels of which were a rather ominous pair of long shining spurs.

"Jade!" He demanded imperiously. "Get the horse loaded up. We shall be late to the meet!" He tapped his hunting whip impatiently against his gleaming boots making a slight scuff mark on the immaculate black leather.

"A please might be nice," muttered Jade under her breath, wishing her head still didn't feel as if it was trapped in a vice. "Best behave yourself today Humphers. That's Gareth, the Major's nephew, riding you today and

I have to say he might be good looking but he's a stuck up pig and he has the manners of a gnat!" She turned to the young man and forced a smile which took a lot of effort to get from her thumping brain onto her face.

"Morning, Your Honour," she said wickedly, sinking into a deep curtsey. "Begging your pardon, Your Worshipfulness, but you won't be needing those spurs on Humphrey!"

"Piss orff!" was the retort. "I always hunt in spurs. What would you know you gothic tart."

"Ooh sir, I don't think 'ow as you should be speaking to us poor servants in that manner. Oi will 'ave to speak to the master."

"Get lost, Jade and load the bloody horse!" Gareth was in no mood for any humour this morning as he, like Jade, also had a huge thumping headache from too much champers at his friend's twenty-first party last night.

"Charmed, I'm sure." Jade loaded Humphrey with a sense of foreboding and wondering how any guy so lovely looking could be such a dick. Life just wasn't fair!

Gareth was a pretty fast driver, used to driving his new Porsche Boxster and he drove the horsebox in the same way. He hurled around the corners and accelerated and decelerated so quickly that Humphrey had all on to stay on his feet. When they arrived at the meet with the nearest thing to a squeal of brakes that a horsebox can produce, Humphrey was unloaded in a muck sweat. Gareth was completely unperturbed and thumped down into the saddle with all the finesse of a sumo mud wrestler and trotted off to the nearest tray of sloe gin for a 'hair of the dog'.

The hunting field eventually moved off, and trotted down the road and as they reached the old turf of the first meadow Humphrey waited for his rider to get his weight forward, touch his reins and squeeze him into canter. Instead all he felt was a huge dig in his flanks with the spurs. Unused to such harsh treatment Humphrey shot forward and leapt in the air, nearly unseating Gareth who responded with, "You bloody old nag," and gave him a sharp slap with his hunting whip.

Humphrey spent the morning galloping and jumping as best he could. Gareth fancied himself as a bit of a rider and kept Humphrey up the front jumping the biggest places so he could show off to all the fit young girls who were following in his wake. Humphrey never minded the galloping and the jumping which he loved, but he found he was hampered at every turn by the unbalanced weight on his back. He found he couldn't jump properly because Gareth held his reins too short and he relied on them to keep his balance in the saddle, consequently Humphrey couldn't stretch his neck and arch his back to clear the fences. Gareth was so busy impressing the impressionable that he galloped Humphrey needlessly (even when hounds weren't running) through deep muddy plough. Humphrey was used to the considerate Major, who would always allow him to walk whenever possible to catch his breath and would never have dreamed of pushing him at top speed through unforgiving deep going.

By two o'clock even the fit Humphrey, hampered by bad riding and reckless galloping, was beginning to feel very tired. Although it was lack of thought rather than wanton cruelty which led Gareth to treat Humphrey as a machine rather than flesh and blood, this did not prevent the unfortunate outcome. So it happened that when Humphrey should have been walking quietly back to the horse box in the gathering gloom at the end of a long and gruelling day, he was spurred into yet another gallop across a rough patch of ground.

A voice rang out through the gloaming. "'Ware bog!"

Humphrey sensed danger and tried to slow his headlong flight but the warning and the sixth sense came too late. He felt his front legs sinking and he floundered into a deep black quagmire. Gareth was sent somersaulting over Humphrey's head to land in a heap with a squelching splat! Humphrey struggled to extricate himself from the clinging suction of the bog but the more he struggled the deeper he sank until the mud rose above his hocks and under his belly. Eventually Humphrey could flounder no more and he lay still. Members of the hunt who had also been riding back to their waggons gathered round in consternation. Gareth looked on helplessly nursing a sprained wrist. With much swearing and grunting, and pushing and pulling, Ted, the local blacksmith (who fortunately had biceps like the incredible hulk) and Tom and Ben, two hefty farmer's sons, slowly but surely, plunge by plunge, managed to move Humphrey to the edge of the bog. Finally, with one supreme push, Humphrey heaved himself onto firmer ground. There he stood, a mass of mud and sweat, white-eyed, head hanging and flanks heaving. Gareth caught up the reins and made to mount.

"Just a minute, young man!" a stern voice ordered, "that horse needs time to recover and to get his wind back. He then needs to be checked to see if he's sound and walked carefully back to the box and taken home."

Gareth looked up into the contemptuous gaze of Lady Smythe, her usually friendly countenance clouded by a look of deep distaste.

"You, young clown! You have given that poor horse an extremely hard day — it looks like Major B's favourite hunter to me. I wouldn't like him to see it now!"

Gareth turned on his heel, picked up the reins and launched himself into the saddle.

"Stupid old bat," he grumbled as he headed Humphrey for the horsebox.

"You need to lead him back!" came floating on the wind, but Gareth, oblivious on an abundance of embarrassment and testosterone, turned a deaf ear. Lady Smythe was left on the lane shaking her head in dismay and muttering a choice of very unladylike words, some of which even Ted the blacksmith had never heard before!

It was after six when the horsebox finally turned through the old stone gateposts and shot up the drive to Eagle Manor. Jade was waiting anxiously in the stable yard.

"Where have you been?" she exclaimed. "We've been so worried. Is everything OK? Haven't you heard of a mobile phone?"

"Forgot it!" Gareth snapped, "Now get that stupid horse unloaded. The daft git only galloped into a bog and threw me off and I've sprained my bloody wrist! How am

I going to play rugby now?" With that he stomped off into the house.

Jade dropped the ramp, peered in at Humphrey and promptly burst into tears. Gone was the cheeky sparkling horse of the morning and in his place was a tired, dejected creature plastered in mud and sweat.

"Humphrey, you poor old lad, what a state you're in. Come on sweetie, let's get you into your nice cosy stable."

Humphrey hobbled slowly and painfully down the ramp, both front legs looking alarmingly outsized.

"Oh, my goodness. What has he done to you?" she wailed. "That idiot, how could he bring you back like this?" Jade wiped her eyes and sniffed loudly to herself. "Come on, gal, get a grip. Pull yourself together! All this blubbing isn't helping the horse!" Jade took a deep breath, sniffed back her tears and wiped her nose furiously on a crumpled tissue which she miraculously found in her pocket amongst the detritus of horse and pony nuts and baler twine. Then she set about the task of righting the wrongs.

"OK, let's get started." She immediately applied ice packs to Humphrey's legs, knowing from her veterinary book that the cold would reduce the bruising and haemorrhaging by restricting the blood flow and constricting any ruptured blood vessels. She then washed Humphrey off in warm water, scraped off the excess, checked him over for injuries and thorns then tucked him up in an anti-sweat rug to dry. She rubbed his ears with a wedge of straw to dry them thoroughly. Half way through these administrations Major B appeared.

"I hear Humphrey's been a real handful today. I wonder wha..." The Major broke off mid-sentence. "Good God! What a mess! What on earth has happened to him? Whoa, my old lad let's have a look at you." The Major inspected Humphrey from head to toe. "Just take those ice packs off Jade and I'll check his legs."

"I was just coming to get you. His legs are rather swollen and I wondered if we might need the vet." Jade removed the ice packs carefully. "Apparently he fell in a bog!"

"A likely story, this horse is the most sure-footed, sensible animal I've ever sat upon! I should think that if he did end up in a bog it would be because he had no choice in the matter and was probably ridden into it full tilt if the truth be known." Major B was definitely not the doddery old fool that some people thought! The Major tut-tutted loudly when he felt the heat and saw the swelling in H's front legs. "Dear, oh dear! Good Lord! Looks to me like he's done in a tendon, certainly on this near fore."

Jade promptly burst into tears for the second time. "It's all my fault I should've taken his spurs off him. I should've followed in the car and made him bring him home when he was tired."

"Now, now, my girl, don't you cry. If blame is to be laid at any door then it is to be at mine. How foolish I was to ever let that crazy young idiot ever near a grand horse like this. By Jove, I'll have his guts for garters. I'll go in now and call the vet. Knowing Colin, he'll come out tonight and give the horse an anti-inflammatory and a pain killer and then maybe we can assess the damage with an ultrasound scan to-morrow." The Major gave Jade a comforting pat on the shoulder. "Now dear, don't you upset yourself. He's a tough lad our Humphrey. If you can continue with the ice packs for another fifteen minutes and then bob pressure bandages on, that will help enormously. Then give him a small feed and lots of hay and get yourself inside and have a cup of tea until the vet comes. I'm going to have a few well-chosen words with that young fool!" And with that he strode off towards the house.

Jade sniffed loudly, perking up slightly at the thought of Colin Peters, the drop-dead gorgeous young vet from their local practice. "Right Humphers, let's make you comfortable and then I'm off to redo my face. It must look a right mess and that Colin Peters is fab." Humphrey blew into her hair spikes and nibbled her jumper, wanting his feed.

Later that evening saw a disconsolate Jade stomping out of the house and into the yard to do evening stables and check up on Humphrey. The vet, not the lovely Colin Peters but some grumpy old git, whose speciality was sheep and who couldn't wait to get home for his tea, had been and gone. He had given H a shot of painkiller and anti- inflammatory with the reassurance that Colin Peters would be back on duty in the morning and would call in then to give the horse a thorough examination.

Mooching into the tack room and turning on the light, Jade's attention was caught by the filthy saddle on the saddle-horse. Needing some occupational therapy to take her mind off the day's traumatic events, She wet a sponge and started to wipe away all the dried mud and dirt. She reached out and angrily and squashed a daddy longlegs that was sitting peacefully, minding its own business, on the end of a saddle rack. Immediately she felt dreadful. Jade would never kill anything, except perhaps the odd fly that was tormenting the horses. She had nearly crashed her car on several occasions avoiding hedgehogs and pheasants and other fauna of North Yorkshire.

"Oh you poor thing, why did I do that? There you were just trying to live your little life and I took it away just because I felt like it."

Jade felt tears coursing down her cheeks and her thoughts turned in their negativity towards the memory of her lovely mum. She could still smell that awful hospital, smell the disinfectant and death on the terminal cancer ward. The cheerful kindness of the nurses the only bright point in the six months of watching her mum getting thinner and weaker as the cancer continued its destructive course. Although it was nearly a year ago, the memory of her mother's brave smile as Jade entered her range of vision was still sharp. The smile that, as the weeks rolled into months, took longer and longer to reach the pale brown eyes. Finally, the smile faded completely and Jade was left sitting by the bedside of a stranger, a vacant bony face of paper-thin skin behind an oxygen mask. Even now Jade could still hear the faint hiss of the oxygen as it was inhaled and exhaled. Tears dropped from the end of Jade's chin and dripped onto the saddle leaving tiny wet circles on the leather.

"Jade dahling! Where are you?" Gareth's plummy accent cut through Jade's misery and a dark shape blocked the doorway. "Oh there you are, old girl! Shirking as usual. I wish I had a cushy job like yours."

Jade turned away, sniffing loudly and rubbed her face on her sleeve, inadvertently catching the small silver hoop in her eyebrow so that her skin burned. Gareth edged closer.

"What on earth is the matter, old thing?" Just popped round to say sorry about Humphers. The old boy is in a fearful strop — banned me from riding big time. He'll come round though eventually, I'm quite sure." Gareth was blessed with an optimistic nature. "Bloody hell! You're crying! I had no idea you were so upset. Must say I feel a bit of a shit myself. Never meant to hurt the old horse."

"I'm not crying just because of Humphrey," Jade bawled "I'm crying cos I've just killed a daddy longlegs."

Jade was now sobbing uncontrollably. Gareth looked at her for a long moment in absolute astonishment and then burst into laughter.

"You've what…?" he stammered between guffaws.

"Oh sod off, you horrible, horrible git!"

Gareth backed up quickly as a can of saddle soap whistled past his left ear.

"Don't you worry, you silly little tart. I'm orff!" Flinging his peace offering carrot on the floor, he stormed off into the night and Jade heard his long strides on the gravel and the screeching of tyres as his Boxster shot out of the yard.

Jade wiped the tear marks off the precious saddle and feeling slightly better, absently went to pick up the can. Noticing the carrot on the floor, she sniffed loudly, squared her shoulders and took it to Humphrey for a late night treat.

Chapter Two

The next morning saw quite a band of people gathering in the yard as Jade took off Humphrey's bandages for further inspection of his forelegs. Even John, the Major's old gardener was pretending to tidy up the flower bed in the corner. His weather-beaten brown face puckered into a frown and he shook his head sadly as he looked at Humphrey's inquisitive face over the stable door. John had a soft spot for Humphrey even though he always claimed his profound dislike of horses. This was because any self-respecting gardener couldn't possibly take to anything that left divots the size of pudding bowls in their immaculate grass verges and was the messiest of all the grazing animals. Well known for leaving green velvet swards in a splodgy mess. For some reason Humphrey didn't seem to feature in this category of grass annihilators and John always went out of his way to give him a pat and usually a carrot when he thought no one was looking. This was favour indeed because getting vegetables from John's care actually onto the dining table was a feat in itself and even Dulcie had to resort to raiding the vegetable garden in the early evening at precisely seven o'clock when John was safely in his cottage watching Emmerdale.

Earlier that morning Jade had found John's bent figure leaning on Humphrey's stable door, tut tutting loudly and proffering several prized carrots.

"Now lass, you know as I'm not partial to 'osses mysel', them being big untidy buggers and land wreckers but this 'oss 'ere — well 'e's different i'nt 'e? 'E's grand 'e is and 'e wouldn't 'urt a fly. Would you? You daft ol' bugger!" H, impervious to words of either praise or scorn, munched appreciatively on his carrot. "I 'ave 't say tho' I don't like look of them legs they look like tree trunks to me!"

"'Ee 'ad a bit of a…" oh no, thought Jade I'm starting to speak like him now! "He had a bit of an accident out hunting yesterday," she explained.

"Aye lass, that may well be but 'e's bin 'unting now for t'Major for two whole seasons and I've never seen 'im in this sorry state afore."

"Ah yes. well Major B wasn't riding him yesterday."

John's eyes opened wide and the bright blue twinkle was lost for a moment behind a veil of concern. "Aye lass, and I bet I know who was doin' the riding — daft young bugger!"

With that final pearl of wisdom, he stomped off to trim the verges of the drive, carefully avoiding the clumps of white snowdrops and the bright spears of green crocus shoots which were destined to be the cheerful yellow and mauve splashes of spring in a few weeks' time.

Major B appeared in Humphrey's stable accompanied by the dishy Colin Peters from The Bishopgarth Veterinary practice. They were closely followed by Lady Smythe, resplendent in her green hunter wellies, waterproof wax jacket and a cascade of pearls.

"Lawrence. Good morning. How are you?" This was for the benefit of the onlookers as Lady Smythe knew exactly how the Major was — having only just left his very large and comfortable four poster bed at five a.m. that morning!

"Ah good morning, Lavinia." The Major shook her hand heartily. "I am feeling exceptionally well this morning thank you. My arthritis seems to have taken a huge turn for the better." Lady Smythe had the grace to blush slightly as her mind rushed unbidden to a vision of the Major in a very un-arthritic position late last night!

This brief exchange was not lost on the rest of the group who, along with most of the village (which included the very rich but very senile Lord Smythe), had known about their liaison for years. Fortunately for them, the village of Little Craven was one of the last bastions of privacy in the whole of the North, where most people either adopted the philosophy of 'live and let live' or had too many skeletons in their own cupboard to risk exposing others.

Lady Smythe reluctantly pushed the image of Lawrence to the back of her mind and with a huge effort, brought her thoughts back to the present.

"Just thought I'd pop in to see how H is. I must say he was in rather a poor state yesterday afternoon. That idiot boy — sorry Lawrence, I know he's your nephew but that doesn't excuse him. That idiot boy rode like a maniac all day and ended up in a bog! He was even going to carry on, until I gave him a roasting! Even then nothing I could say would dissuade him from riding the poor horse back to the wagon when everybody could see he was as lame as a crow."

Major B had heard this story during the night and an image of Lavinia in her pearls and not much else came unbidden to his mind. He also reluctantly pushed this enchanting image away to be retrieved later at a more suitable time and furrowed his brow in concentration to return to the matters in hand.

"Ah well it's good to hear the truth at last. He seems to have lost his way that young man. I really am at a loss as to what to do with him. But I do know one thing, that's the last time he will ever sit on one of my horses. According to Gareth it was all the horse's fault of course. He tried to tell me that my favourite hunter was unschooled and dangerous. Never heard such poppycock in all my life," snorted the Major in disgust.

Jade, knowing the signs of the Major 'going off on one' as she so eloquently described his occasional tirades, took this timely opportunity to stand Humphrey before them. Everyone stood patiently in silence as Colin made a thorough examination of H's front legs.

"Well!" he proclaimed finally. "I'm afraid it looks like the main problem is damage to the digital flexor tendon on the near fore. I will give him a shot of anti-inflammatory and a painkiller for now and come back with my ultrasound equipment tomorrow so I can diagnose the situation exactly. He will need hot and cold therapy on those legs for five to six days, continued pressure bandaging and more anti-inflammatory drugs for a while. He needs to be kept on box rest until the swelling is controlled and then he can begin gentle exercise starting with walking in hand for ten minutes twice daily for a month. This will be a long job I'm afraid and will require lots of patience and TLC."

There was a long silence broken finally by Lady Smythe.

"Colin, what is the long-term prognosis? Will he ever be sound again?"

"He should be sound eventually but he'll probably never stand up to a lot of hard days hunting and certainly not in the near future. Hacking and the occasional day, yes, but not twice a week for a whole season."

"Oh dear me," sighed the Major, patting Humphrey's neck tenderly. "I feared as much. Well it's a long gentle uphill slope for you, my lad, and then we will have to see what is to be done." Humphrey stood quietly enjoying the attention, totally unaware that his fate was being discussed and decided upon. Jade felt tears welling up and fought hard to keep them back.

"You will keep him, Major, won't you?"

"Well unfortunately he won't fit my bill anymore." Lavinia fixed him a piercing stare. "However," he continued rapidly, "we have had such marvellous times together and I am so fond of the old boy we'll find a slot for him somewhere. Maybe you can help Lavinia?"

Lavinia smiled, reaffirming to herself why she still adored this man after all these years.

"Of course I'll help. I'll spread the word. Actually, I'll call my sister Annabel. She's looking for a quiet hack to ride out with the children. I must say she seems to have lost her nerve a bit so H would be just the thing. I'll ask her if she can wait until the summer hols when the children are back from school. He would have a marvellous home there. I could keep an eye on him and I know they would love and adore him."

"I do hope so," mumbled Jade, feeling in her heart that no one could possible look after him and love him as much as she did.

H's dilemma having been satisfactorily concluded, everyone adjourned to The Manor to warm the cold morning with cups of coffee, laced with whisky. Colin Peters then left to continue his rounds before the whisky overtook the coffee around the large pine table in the comfortable AGA-warm kitchen.

Jade meanwhile tenderly rebandaged Humphrey's legs and gave him a huge net of hay.

"Oh Humphers, I'm so sorry that this had to happen to you. You're such a sweetie, you never deserved this. I could kill that stupid Gareth! What a plonker! I hope I never set eyes on him again." Jade pushed a finger down the inside of H's bandages just to check that they weren't too tight. "I'm sure that you'll be very happy though with Lady Smythe's sister. They'll look after you and they're only half an hour away. I'll be able to bob across to see you now and then. But you will have to be very patient now for a few weeks and not get stroppy cos you will have to stay in your box for quite a while." Jade knew she was prattling but it made her feel better and H flicked his ears back and forth as he munched his hay, liking the sound of her voice.

Gradually winter waned and the days lengthened and became warmer and a golden army of daffodils began to replace the humble snowdrops and blazing crocuses guarding the drive. Humphrey was recovering well and was allowed on the horse walker building up to two twenty-minute sessions a day.

About this time a new face was seen looking over the spare loose box door. A big grey face with a slightly Roman nose. This was to be Major B's new hunter for next season. Eventually as spring progressed both horses were turned out in the five-acre field at the bottom of the drive. The exuberant grey would canter round and round bucking and cavorting with tail streaming like a white flag. He would screech to a halt, bounce on all fours like a giant Tigger and then begin the whole process again! H's tendon damage slowly repaired and the swelling in his limbs reduced. His near fore would always show a slight thickening, but by mid-summer, with much rejoicing from everyone, Colin Peters declared Humphrey to be one hundred percent sound.

One bright morning in July when Jade went to the five acres on her daily inspection of the horses she found to her surprise Gareth, looking resplendent in black leathers, leaning on the paddock rail. A tell-tale carrot was just visible in his back pocket and a mass of gleaming metal in the shape of a new Harley-Davidson Breakout was by his side.

The last time Jade had seen him was at the Hunt Ball a few months ago. He had been standing at the champagne bar with the clinging form of the glamorous Louisa Langley-Fox draped all over him. Jade had quickly headed in the other direction towards the bar to swig pints of lager with boyfriend Dan, and his rowdy mates.

"What on earth are you doing here?" she asked sharply. What a gorgeous bike, she thought dreamily.

"Well that's a lovely greeting! I'm very well thank you for asking and how are you, Jade, on this beautiful morning?"

"Don't be so bloody facetious. I'm not in the mood" she retorted.

"Oooh big word. More than two syllables. Where did you learn that?"

"Get lost, you dickhead!"

Gareth just had to laugh. He couldn't help himself.

"OK, OK, let's start again, shall we? Good morning, Jade. You're looking very lovely this morning, if I might say so." Jade looked at him in surprise, suspecting sarcasm but could find none.

"Actually, I'm very well, thank you," she replied politely, managing to strangle the customary 'your honour' and deciding to give the curtsey a miss. "And to what do we owe the pleasure of your presence amongst us this beautiful morning?"

"Actually I have come to see how old Humphers is progressing. I have been a few times actually when I thought the coast was clear. Contrary to popular opinion I do feel bad about being responsible for his injuries. I think I must have had far too many shots of whiskey mac and sloe gin."

"That's no excuse, you thoughtless idiot! Actually he's doing fine. He's sound now and is going to Lady

Smythe's sister, Annabel, at the end of this month for light hacking."

"That's marvellous! I did ask Mama if we could have him in retirement at home with us, if push came to shove and he had nowhere to go."

Jade wondered how anyone could abuse a horse and then do an about turn and be concerned for its future welfare.

"Because I feel guilty, you twit!" Gareth must have read her thoughts. "Come on then, use your magical horse whispering powers and get the old boy over."

"HUMPHREY!" yelled Jade in her best parade ground roar. Gareth put his hands over his ears in mock horror!

"Gawd, girl, you've a voice like a fog horn!"

Humphrey raised his head, gave them a languid stare and then carried on eating. However, the big grey at his side threw up his head, whinnied loudly and galloped fly-bucking and kicking full tilt towards them. Just when it looked as if he would crash into the paddock rail, he performed an immaculate handbrake turn and bounced to a standstill with much head tossing and snorting.

"Wow!" gasped Gareth in admiration. "What is that?"

"That," said Jade primly, "is entirely your fault! That is Cockatoo, Cocky for short, Major B's new hunter. He is fabulous, isn't he, but he's as daft as a brush! We're hoping he might settle down — eventually."

"Well girl — wrong whisper — wrong horse!"

Jade giggled. "You're right, that was a fat lot of good. Come on then you'll have to get some dirt on those posh biker boots. Follow me."

They tramped across the meadow in companionable silence only stopping occasionally to shoo Cocky away to a respectable distance. Jade found herself trying hard to fend off any feeling of attraction towards the tall, long-striding guy at her side. She didn't even like him! What was it about him? The faint smell of leather and Jean Paul Gautier, or his tall presence making her feel small and secure? Her mind flew unbidden back to pleasant memories of the long walks with her father when she was a child. Jade let out an involuntary sigh. Oh yes, she thought, her precious father who, six months after her mother's death, shacked up with the lovely Melissa, not much older than herself. How could he! Jade, still raw with grief, bewildered, watched her father falling in lust with this overgrown schoolgirl. The spate of piercings and drunken nights in the pub increased in frequency and intensity until the final straw. The night that Melissa took that dreadful empty space in her father's bed and Jade, who could stay no longer, fled to her Aunt Dulcie at The Manor.

Jade, sunk deep in thought, stumbled on a rough tussock of grass and felt a gentle but firm hand on her elbow.

"Steady up, you daft tart. You're not looking where you're going."

Jade, quite liking the feel of his strong arm supporting her and the closeness of him, bit back a waspish retort.

“Thank you, you’re right. I was busy day dreaming.”

“Penny for them?” asked Gareth, but they had reached Humphrey and Jade pretended she hadn’t heard him. Gareth shrugged and gave Humphrey his carrot which he munched greedily, lazily flicking flies from his glossy rump.

“Gosh, he looks well.” Gareth ran a practised hand down Humphrey’s near fore. “Swellings down, just a slight thickening around that digital flexor.” Jade looked at him in amazement.

“I didn’t think you knew diddly squat about horses.”

“Actually I have been playing polo since I was eleven. We’ve had polo ponies break down before. Only one,” he added hastily, trying to block Jade’s retort.

“Not surprising the way you ride!”

“Mater wanted me to play professionally but my first love is cars and bikes. They want me to take over the finance company eventually but it’s so boring. All that managing of money, it drives me mad. I don’t even care about money!”

“That’s all very well for you to say cos you’ve got loads. What star sign are you?” asked Jade.

“Pisces, why?”

“Ah well” Jade nodded wisely, “that’s the reason. Pisces hate dealing with all things financial. It’s anathema to them.”

“How on earth do you know that?”

“Because I am one!”

“Oh well, can’t argue with that. Have to go now.” They made their way back across the field to the drive.

"Would you like a lift back to the house on Maxine?" Gareth broke the companionable silence.

"Maxine!" Jade exclaimed incredulously.

"The bike! Mad Max the biker — Mel Gibson then Tom Hardy, *Mad Max – Fury Road.* That's me and that's Maxine, my lean mean machine!"

"Little boys and their toys," muttered Jade.

"What's that?"

"Don't mind if I do actually." Jade was as nonchalant as possible. "It'll save me a walk back and I've lots to do. Fences to creosote and…"

"Yeah yeah, people to see, places to go. I know the feeling! Come along then hop on."

Jade settled on the pillion seat behind Gareth, wrapped her arms round his waist and felt the broad muscles of his back against her breasts. A surge of energy swept through her and she had to fight hard not to shiver. They shot up the field lane and turned left into the long, gravelled drive, the Harley accelerating with a whoosh that had Jade hanging on for dear life. Gareth, showing off, executed a skidding turn into the stable yard and screeched to a halt.

"Wow — that was great!" exclaimed Jade swinging her leg over the back of the seat. She just couldn't keep the excitement out of her voice and forgot all about remaining cool and unimpressed.

"Most girls I know would be a quivering wreck after that."

"Well obviously I'm not like most girls you know!"

Gareth looked into Jade's sparkling eyes and a faint smile escaped his lips.

"Obviously. And hey, maybe you're not such a daft tart after all." With that, he bent down and touched her lips softly with his and then was gone. Jade, alone in the yard, listened until the huge cacophony of sound faded into the distance and then, feeling uncharacteristically pleased with herself, bounced into the tack room to find the creosote.

Chapter Three

A week later a very smart blue Range Rover and trailer appeared in the stable yard at The Manor. No sooner had it drawn to a standstill than out of the door tumbled two young girls. In appearance as alike as two peas in a pod, with pale blonde hair swept up into pony tails and denim jodhpurs slightly wrinkled on long coltish legs.

"Where is he, where is he?" they screeched in unison. "Come on, Mummy. Is this him? Is it? Is it?"

"Sam, Charlie! For goodness sake calm down!" admonished their mother as she alighted gracefully from the driver's seat. "The poor horse will be frightened to death with you two shouting all over the place."

Humphrey's head appeared over the stable door and he flicked his ears back and forth as he listened to the commotion.

"Oooh Mummy, I hope this is him. Isn't he beautiful!" cried Sam reaching up on tip toes to pat Humphrey's nose.

"Oooh, but he's soooo big. Is this him?" Charlie gazed up at Humphrey's head in awe. "He's a lot bigger than Marshmallow, isn't he Mummy?"

"No, he isn't!" said Sam knowingly. Samantha was born four minutes earlier than Charlotte and felt that this gave her the right to be a) far more knowledgeable than her sister and b) disagree with everything she said.

Although identical twins physically, mentally they were very non-identical! Sam, at nine years old had confidence and dogmatism beyond her years, whilst Charlie, timid and shy, was still very much following in the wake of her only just, elder sister.

"Well he looks a lot bigger, doesn't he Mummy?" On this occasion Charlie was not to be deterred.

"Yes dear," replied her mother patiently. "Humphrey is far bigger than Marshmallow."

"He's not as big as Snowflake though." Sam was determined to have the last word.

"Yes, he is!" stormed Charlie.

"Isn't!"

"Is!"

"Stop it, girls, stop it! Humphrey is much bigger than both your ponies so kindly let's put the matter to rest. I'm so sorry," she turned to Jade. "I'm Annabel Lawson, Lady Smythe's sister. I hope you're expecting us. You must be Jade. I've heard lots of good things about you from Lavinia and the Major. I don't know what he'd do without you." Jade blushed, unused to such compliments and took the proffered hand on which two very large diamonds glinted in the sunlight.

"Oh yes, we are expecting you," she stammered, quite transfixed by the bling. "Wow are they real?"

"To tell you the truth these are zircon. We had copies made of the real thing. They are in the safe at the bank — too precious to wear! Silly really but I just don't feel confident wearing thousands of pounds on my fingers. What if I lost one? My husband George would go mad!"

Jade, who had just lost her favourite pewter ring with the snake's head on it in the muck heap that very morning, the ring that Dan had given her for her birthday, nodded understandingly. She hadn't quite worked out yet how she was going to broach the subject to him.

"Well do come and meet Humphrey. I do hope you like him. He is the nicest horse I have ever had to look after and fabulous to ride." Jade felt the tears welling up and tried desperately to stop them but one disobeyed and managed to escape, trickling slowly down her cheek. "Sorry," she choked. "I'm just so fond of him but I'm so glad that you're having him and he's going to a good home."

"Now don't you worry, dear," Jade felt a comforting arm around her shoulder and instantly felt her mum's presence somewhere near. "We will look after him and love him. All our animals are part of the family and dreadfully spoilt. After all, he's only going a few miles down the road. You must come over and help me to get used to him and you can ride him yourself whenever you want. I am nothing like as brave as Lavinia. I just like to go out for a quiet hack and Major B says he'll be just the thing. He is rather beautiful isn't he?" She gazed at Humphrey with the appreciation of a connoisseur of beautiful things whether inanimate or alive, and gently stroked his nose. "What do you think girls?"

The girls were already in Humphrey's box, oohing and aahing and cuddling him.

"Oh Mummy, we love him, we love him. He's like a big brown bear," said Charlie ecstatically.

"No he isn't, you twit. He's a furry 'my little pony'." argued Sam.

"No he isn't!" screamed Charlie and immediately began to cry.

"If you two don't shut up," Jade couldn't help herself, "you will frighten Humphrey. He gets very upset at loud noises. He doesn't like crying, and," she added sternly, "he won't want to go home with you."

"Well said," whispered Annabel.

The girls immediately looked forlorn and proceeded to speak to each other in loud stage whispers.

"Get off him, it's my turn to cuddle him. You go and cuddle the other side," ordered Sam.

"OK," whispered her twin meckly and promptly crawled under Humphrey's stomach.

"Oh my goodness." Annabel was horrified. "Oh thank goodness he's so quiet."

"That was very very silly and dangerous!" scolded Jade, knowing that as a child she did the very same thing. "It doesn't matter how quiet and kind Humphrey is. If something startled him he might stand on you and hurt you without meaning to. He can't see you when you're down there."

Fortunately, Major B arrived at that moment with offers of fruit juice and cakes and the twins, without any further ado, followed him and their mother up to the house.

Old John appeared from nowhere and produced a carrot.

"Bye old lad. Never bin one for 'osses m'sel', but I'll miss you, I will." He stroked Humphrey's smooth neck with his gnarled old fingers and Humphrey gently took the proffered carrot. Jade sniffed loudly, "Now, now, don't fret y'sel', lass. I can tell them there folks 'll look after 'im proper like and 'e'll be staying in't family so to speak." Jade gulped, groped for her crumpled tissue amongst the crumbs of pony nuts in her pocket and led Humphrey towards the waiting trailer.

He looked a picture of health, a vibrant mix of colour as the sunlight reflected off the sheen of his conker-coloured coat. His black legs and the glossy ebony of his mane and tail gleaming in sharp contrast against the bright bay body.

Major B and the others returned just as H was being loaded.

"Well, Jade, my dear, he looks marvellous, just like his old self." He gave Humphrey an affectionate pat. "Goodbye, old man. Be good. We will come and see you often."

Humphrey walked confidently up the ramp and with the meekness of all animals who trust in the decisions of their masters, stood quietly as the breeching strap was clipped across and the ramp was swung up with a dull thud. Jade, meanwhile, fastened the lead rope with a quick release knot and gave him a last hug.

"I'm coming to see you in a few days, old man. You'll have such a lovely lazy life."

The stark irony of these words was not yet known to her. Humphrey snorted gently and, as usual, blew into the black gelled spikes that passed as hair.

Jade, John and the Major watched the Range Rover and trailer move slowly out of the stable yard and down the drive. John rubbed his eyes on the rough sleeve of his old knitted jumper, muttering under his breath.

"Can't stand 'osses m'sel' and this damn sun's makin' me eyes water!" With that he turned away and trudged disconsolately towards the solace of his kitchen garden. Jade went into the tack room and proceeded to cry her eyes out and the Major went into his study and poured himself a very large whiskey.

Humphrey's new home was a large roomy loose box and a four-acre field which he shared with the twins' two ponies, Marshmallow and Snowflake. Marshmallow, Charlie's pony, was strawberry roan in colour, a rather portly pony on short legs which could easily have starred in one of Thelwell's cartoons. The dapple-grey Snowflake was much more a thoroughbred, slimmer version. Annabel's husband George, in one of his lighter moments, had compared them to a Fiat and a Ferrari which Sam found immensely funny but Charlie needless to say, did not. Marshmallow had a thick wiry mane, which no matter how often Charlie tried to lay it down with a damp brush, always sprang back up in the air like a great ginger wire brush. Snowflake, however, had a fine silky mane as befitting her breeding but just loved being as dirty as possible and was happiest when she was caked in mud and grime with not a white hair to be seen.

At first the ponies were quite affronted by the big bay intruder in their lives and kept him at a distance with bared teeth and flashing hooves. However, Humphrey just ignored them and kept out of their way. As the days wore on they became accustomed to his presence and even whinnied after him when he went out without them.

To begin with, Annabel rode Humphrey only in the small sand arena and although she was a kind and considerate rider, she felt very nervous. Humphrey, however, was so laid back, he just plodded along, never shying once at the birds flapping in the hedge or giving any hint of the odd buck which he used to put in with the Major when he was hunting fit. After a couple of weeks and with some lessons from Jade, Annabel became much more confident and began to feel completely at home on the big bay horse. She started to hack out with the twins and actually began to set her fears aside and enjoy herself.

Very occasionally, after a lot of nagging, the twins were allowed to ride Humphrey in the arena under her watchful eye. Sam being Sam immediately kicked Humphrey into a trot and with a, "Look at me, Mummy," and ponytail flying managed rising trot for two whole circuits before Humphrey decided that walking was less of an effort. Charlie, however, just walked Humphrey sedately round the track, pretending she was Jade who was her heroine at the moment and asking her horrified mother, "When can I have my ears and eyebrow and lip pierced like Jade, Mummy? It looks so cool."

One drizzling grey morning, when Humphrey had been in his new home for about four weeks, the twins appeared in the stables and with much huffing and puffing brushed their ponies, tacked them up and waited impatiently for their mother.

"Wish she'd hurry up," said Sam crossly. "Tell you what, why don't we tack up Humph ourselves? It'll save loads of time and I know which saddle and bridle are his." No sooner said than done! Sam disappeared, returning triumphantly a few moments later with the saddle across her arms and the bridle in a tangled trail around her boots.

"He's too big," cried Charlie. "I can't even reach his head. How can we put his bridle over those high-up ears?"

"You're such a scaredy cat. I am going to fetch that chair from the tack room and climb on it. He isn't that big anyway. He's not much bigger than Snowflake." Before a repeat argument of relative heights could ensue, Sam ran off to the tack room and returned dragging an old wooden chair which had most definitely seen better days. Humphrey snorted in alarm as she scraped the rickety chair across the cobbles and with a great struggle managed to manoeuvre it through the stable door and set it down by his shoulder.

"Right!" she puffed. "Now I'll stand on the chair and you hand me the bridle. Come on, I know how this fits." Humphrey stood patently whilst she tried desperately to sort out the tangled mass of leather. Eventually she managed to place the bit in Humphrey's accommodating mouth and loop the rest of the bridle round one ear.

"That doesn't look quite right!" volunteered Charlie. "I think we should wait for Mummy."

"Of course it's right. Now hand me up the saddle," Sam demanded with all the confidence of the 'ignorance is bliss' syndrome. With much pulling from Sam and pushing from Charlie, the pair of them managed to get the saddle half way up Humphrey's side. Then suddenly as Sam gave a final heave, the frail chair leg gave way at the joint and buckled inwards. Sam overbalanced, the chair collapsed and saddle, chair and child ended up in a mass of legs and leather on top of the squawking Charlie.

"Ouch! Get off! Get off me! You great twit," she screamed.

Humphrey, bridle hanging from one ear, added to the melee by leaping sideways and shooting over to the far corner of the stable where he stood snorting loudly in mock terror.

Fortunately, at that very moment, Annabel appeared at the stable door.

"Sam, Charlie, are you all right? Oh my goodness! What on earth has happened?" She quickly managed to extricate the twins from the chaos.

"She fell on my leg!" shrieked Charlie. "She did it on purpose."

"No I didn't. It was an accident, Mummy. We were trying to be helpful and tack up Humph for you."

"Well girls. He's just a bit too big for you to manage."

"That's what I said," sniffed Charlie.

"You're such a little creep," retorted Sam, sticking her tongue out at her twin. "We were doing really well until that fucking chair collapsed!"

Annabel blanched. "What did you say?"

"I said we were doing really well until that fu..."

"Stop right there, young lady. Where did you learn language like that?"

"Susie Yates says it all the time."

"Yes, well it's a bad swear word and Susie Yates is a very naughty girl."

"Jade says it too," offered Charlie proudly.

"Well Jade is much older than Susie Yates but even so it's not a very nice word."

"Daddy says it all the time too." Sam was not going to be outdone.

"Right girls. That will do!" Annabel realised she was fighting a losing battle. "Sam, for being so rude, you will forfeit your ride out this morning and you will untack your pony right now and then go into the house and help Mrs Turner with the dusting."

"But Mummy!"

"No buts — off you go."

Sam, muttering furiously to herself, untacked Snowflake, and stomped off with a face like thunder, sticking her tongue out again at Charlie as she passed.

Annabel untangled the bridle, retrieved the hapless saddle, soothed Humphrey and in no time at all she and Charlie were mounted and riding uneventfully out of the yard.

Ten minutes later they were walking down the grassy track heading into Thornthwaite Forest.

The sky had cleared to a brilliant blue and flies buzzed noisily around the horses' heads.

"These beastly flies!" exclaimed Annabel. "It doesn't matter how much fly spray we put on it never seems to have any effect."

"Let's trot then, Mummy, then we can leave them behind." Charlie urged the puffing Marshmallow forward.

Soon the only sound to be heard was the rhythmical thud of hooves on the springy grass and as they entered the forest, the dark conifers blocked the sunlight into bright shafts and the track narrowed down to a single path.

"Come on, Mummy, let's canter!" Charlie pushed Marshmallow into canter and leant forward over her pony's shoulder pretending to be Zara Tindall whom she had seen on TV going cross-country. The forest was dark and cool after the warmth of the sun and the trees closed in as tall sentinels guarding the ever-narrowing track. Soon the soft drumming of the hoofbeats increased in frequency until the three time beats of the steady canter changed stealthily into the four fast beats of the gallop.

"Steady, Charlie, not so fast!" shouted Annabel as she tried to steady Humphrey who was snatching at the reins in excitement, remembering his hunting days galloping down similar tracks following another horse in just this fashion. "Whoa, boy, steady there," she soothed. Gradually Humphrey settled into a long striding gallop and Annabel, balanced with her weight slightly out of the saddle, leant forward and felt the thrill and exhilaration of the power underneath her and the rush of wind in her face.

Suddenly she realised they were approaching a blind bend in the track at frightening speed and a horrifying sense of danger kicked in.

"Slow down! SLOW DOWN!" she yelled frantically to Charlie but the noise of the wind and another more ominous, mechanical sound drowned her words. Annabel's heart seemed to jump and pound furiously in her chest. A motorbike. Oh heavens, no, not in here! "Charlie! Charlie! STOP!" She screamed and hauled on Humphrey's reins. The adrenaline pumped round by her hammering heart gave her a power and authority she was unaware of and he started to slow down.

Charlie and Marshmallow shot round the corner and were confronted by a huge silver and black motorbike filling the narrow path and hurtling towards them. For a brief moment Charlie clocked the look of horror on the young man's face under his helmet as he tried to brake. She felt her pony slipping and sliding underneath her and a smack on her knee as Marshmallow dived left into the trees, then a floor of pine needles rushed up to meet her.

Humphrey tried desperately to check his speed as the shiny monster skidded and fell across his path in a wheel-spinning, shrieking mass of metal. Annabel, in a daze of horror, felt his muscles bunch underneath her as with a tremendous leap he sprang into the air, trying to avoid the carnage before him. She hung on grimly and for the briefest of instants thought she would remain in the saddle but her flagging grip was no match for Humphrey's explosive power and she felt herself ejected upwards. A huge crack reverberated in her skull and then there was nothing.

Charlie lay on the damp forest floor where she fell, winded and crying with shock. Out of the corner of one eye she could just make out an unperturbed Marshmallow who, thinking of food as usual, was snuffling for grass amongst the moss and pine needles. Slowly her recollection dawned and she stood up gingerly and looked up the track to where her mother lay. She was partly hidden in the wood, her body at a very peculiar angle at the base of a large spruce tree.

"Mummy! Mummy!" she screamed, running to her side. "Get up! Get UP!" Charlie started to sob hysterically and was about to lift the still head when a deep male voice interrupted her.

"NO! NO! STOP!" it commanded. "Whatever you do, do not touch her. It might make things worse." She turned to see a young man staring at her from beneath the wrecked bike. His face was ashen and twisted in pain.

"My mummy won't speak. She won't move. She's dead! What happened to her! I know she's dead!" Charlie was hysterical.

"Look kid. You will have to get a grip," stammered Gareth, trying to make his voice sound stern in an attempt to override the pain which now threatened to swamp him. It was unlike anything he had ever experienced and was sweeping up the whole of his left leg in ferocious blasts. The words seem to be floating about in his head and he heard them from far off. "Your mum is not dead." Oh God, how he hoped that was true. "But we must get some help immediately. Now stop that noise at once and come and help me with this bike. I can't seem to move my leg." Gareth, through his nausea and dizziness, glanced down at his leg which was trapped under the bike and was positioned at an alarming angle. He thought he could see a metal spoke and a flash of white bone protruding from his ripped leather trousers and immediately felt another wave of dizziness engulf him.

"You're Gareth, aren't you?" screamed Charlie accusingly. "You've killed my mummy. I hate you and I'm glad you've hurt your leg." Her thoughts, with the clear justice of the very young, came straight to her lips.

She pulled at the bike with her tiny frame and sobbed loudly. “I can’t move this thing. It’s a stupid old bike.” She gave it a swift kick. “I hate it and I hate YOU!” she screamed. The screaming and the movement of the bike’s spoke against the exposed bone brought Gareth back from the edge of the comforting black abyss of unconsciousness where he was teetering and preparing to fall. Charlie’s small fingers clawed at his arm. “Get up! Get UP!” she yelled into the still grey face. “Open your eyes!” Gareth’s eyes flickered open and he saw the tear-streaked big eyes looming out of the fog that surrounded him.

“Look kid!” he whispered. “This is no good. I can’t get up because my leg is broken. If you kick the bike one more time I shall be unconscious and unable to help. So cut it out. You will have to get on your pony and go for help. Wait!” A surge of endorphins allowed him to think more clearly. “Feel in my pocket for my mobile phone.” She felt in the leather bomber jacket pocket and produced a squashed travesty of a mobile. Once again she burst into tears. “Right” said Gareth. “That’s no use. You will have to be a good kid and get on your pony and go for help.”

Charlie straightened up, wiped her nose on her sleeve. “OK. I’ll go get Marshmallow.” She headed off the track, stooping under the low branches towards her pony but was brought to a sudden stop with a gasp of horror. “Oh no! Not you too!” Marshmallow was resting his off hind leg and there was a jagged tear across his thigh where the brake handle of the bike had gouged him as he hurtled through the gap. Charlie just couldn’t stop crying. She felt as if her whole world was falling in pieces around her. Everyone was hurt so badly. Her mum, Gareth and now Marshmallow. She sank to the ground and sobbed and sobbed until her breath came in short rasps. How could such a lovely day end like this? Through her despair she heard a feeble moan.

"Come on, kid, pull yourself together. Hurry up!"

"My pony's cut his leg and I can't ride him. What shall I do?"

"Ride the other one, you twit," came the terse answer. "You will have to go back the way you have come. It will take far too long if you carry on to the end of the forest and back by the road. Look kid, you don't have a choice. You need to get help for your mother as soon as possible. You must go back the same way you came. Take my jacket and put it over her. Come on, hurry up."

Charlie managed to tug the leather bomber jacket from the wincing Gareth and ran to place it tenderly over the still prostrate form of her mother. She shivered as suddenly the sun's rays filtering through the trees lost all their warmth and the dark trees seemed menacingly close.

"How will I get past you both?" she wailed. "You're in the way. H is too big to get under the fir tree branches to go round you."

"You'll just have to walk Humphrey around your mum as best you can and then jump over me and the bike and gallop back home as fast as you can." The words sounded ridiculous even to Gareth as he uttered them.

She was aghast. "What if we step on you? What if I fall off?"

"Enough of the 'What ifs', kid." The young man forced a ghost of a smile. "I'll close my eyes and pray that you don't land on my broken leg. Now get going!"

Charlie gulped and gazed at Humphrey who was standing patiently, his reins snared on a branch. She walked quietly towards him and he looked up expectantly as she called his name. All of a sudden he seemed to have grown to nineteen hands, a veritable giant of a horse.

"But he's so big. I'm frightened! How will I get on?" Panic and despair overwhelmed her and she began to sob again. Although it had only been a few minutes since the accident she felt as if whole hours had passed.

Gareth also lost his sense of time. He knew he had been lying under his bike for a lifetime and felt himself slipping in and out of a black void.

"Just lead Humphrey up to the bike," he croaked. "Stand on the wheel, try and lengthen your stirrup as far as it will go and then scramble up."

Charlie grasped Humphrey's rein and just managed to turn him towards the bike in the tight confines of the narrow track. She led him very carefully past the prostrate form of her mother. Humphrey snorted as he passed the prone figure but stepped carefully over the still legs. Charlie heaved a sigh of relief and led Humphrey as close as possible to the metal tangle. It took her some time, with shaking fingers, to alter the buckle on the stiff leather and let the stirrup down as far as it would go. She balanced precariously on the wheel, which moved as she did so. Gareth let out an anguished cry and then was still.

With a great heave she managed to scramble up Humphrey's side and flung her leg across the saddle.

"I've made it I've made it!" she cried out to Gareth, but there was no reply. For a moment she struggled with the stirrup leathers to try and shorten them but from above she just couldn't manage to move the tight buckles.

"Leave those. Pick up your reins kid and give him a big kick, you haven't much room." Gareth made a tremendous effort to stay awake. She picked up the thick rubber reins in her small fingers and curled her fists around them. They seemed very stiff and inflexible in her hand rather like the unwieldy handlebars of her new bike and not a bit like reins. She squeezed Humphrey along the track towards her mother and then pulling on the right rein slowly turned him towards Gareth and the bike.

"There's no room!" she wailed. "How can I do it from here?"

"C'mon kid! I know you can do it." Gareth's voice was barely a whisper and his eyes needed no bidding as they closed involuntarily. Nature's gentle caress overwhelmed him and with that final word of encouragement he slipped back into oblivion.

Charlie felt her heart pounding in her chest and fear made her feel sick.

"Oh help, I feel so scared." She glanced back at her mother's still shape and gritted her teeth in determination. "C'mon, Humph. This is it!" With that she slapped him on the neck hard with the heavy reins and gave him the biggest kick she could muster with her short legs. Humphrey shot forward then slowed down to look at the strange obstacle in his path. He had jumped many things out hunting but never anything like this. He ground to a halt. Charlie screaming at him in frustration, gave him another kick and yet another slap with the reins.

Humphrey, recognising that these strange kicking signals were similar to the ones that the Major occasionally gave him when they were in a tight spot out hunting, did his Harrier Jump Jet impression. He shot into the air, clearing the boy and the bike with ease. His diminutive rider was ejected swiftly from the saddle and for the second time in the space of a few minutes, hit the deck with a crunch. She rose slowly and was surprised to find that she was unhurt. With grim determination written all over her tear-stained face she collected Humphrey and led him wearily back to the bike. Gareth was very still but opened a bloodshot eye as she stood again on the wobbling wreckage.

"You did it girl!" he whispered. "You are a star. Now ride as fast as you can. GO!"

Charlie scrambled back into the saddle and pushed for canter back down the track. Her sense of urgency through her adrenalin and flying reins and thumping legs reached through to Humphrey and they galloped down the track in a whirl of flying dust. It was a nightmare journey, a far cry from the gentle trot in the safety of the manège. Charlie could feel the power of the big horse beneath her. She could hardly see for the tears, which for some reason just would not stop, but she leant forward and tried to ignore the blur of the ground beneath her. She hung on to Humphrey's mane like grim death.

"Don't fall off! Don't fall off!" The vivid picture of her mother lying under the fir tree flashing in her mind made her clench her jaw and she clutched the hairs fiercely until her fingers hurt with the effort. She repeated the mantra in her brain, "Must stay on! Must stay on! Take me home! Take me home!" hoping that if she said it often enough, it would come true.

Humphrey shot out of the forest and, totally out of control, headed down the road for home. Charlie prayed that there would be no cars in the way and fate smiled on her and granted her at least that prayer.

Humphrey hurtled down the road and galloped towards home. His steel shoes flashed sparks as, swerving into the drive, they struck the flinty stones in the entrance. The noise heralded his arrival and the front door was flung open by a worried Mrs Turner, the Lawson's cleaner, with Sam at her side. Humphrey stood with his head low and white flecks of foam dripped from his shoulders onto the floor.

"Oh no!" screamed Sam. "What has happened? Charlie, are you OK? What have you done to poor Humphrey? Where's Mummy?"

Mrs Turner took a sprightly step forward and caught the exhausted Charlie in her arms as she rolled down Humphrey's heaving sides.

"Mummy's hurt in the forest. Motorbike came — horrible, rode home — Mummy's hurt badly," she gasped. "She might be dead!" Her gasp rose to a wail and both she and Sam started to howl. Amidst the cacophony Mrs Turner, never one to panic and with four children of her own, promptly took charge.

"Right, girls. This is NOT helping!" she said firmly. "So let's get organised. I will call an ambulance. Sam, you will look after this poor horse and Charlie, you will come with me and try to tell me whereabouts you were in the forest when it all happened. She then half carried Charlie into the house and Humphrey was led away by a tearful Sam to the stables. Sam — who was very slowly, reading Black Beauty and having reached the bit when he was ridden hard to fetch the doctor and was given too much to drink afterwards, caught colic and nearly died — was very careful to give Humphrey only a small drink of tepid water, some hay to munch on and a deep bed of straw.

Meanwhile, unfortunately, Charlie could not accurately relay to Mrs Turner on which track the accident happened so in her wisdom, Mrs Turner got Charlie to take her to the edge of the forest where the ride had begun. The ambulance arrived and Charlie then managed to lead the ambulance down the track. Finally, the forest track narrowed, making any further progress of the ambulance impossible. Charlie then led Mrs Turner, the medics and their stretcher down into the forest following deep hoof prints and hoping fervently that these were the right hoof prints on the right track. It seemed an age before she rounded that dreadful bend and caught sight of a prone figure and the mangled bike. She shot forward and running as fast as she could, stumbled over the inert Gareth, scrambled over the bike and headed towards her mother. She ignored the shouts to stop from the medics and arrived breathlessly at her side.

"Mummy! Mummy! Are you all right? Mummy, I made it! I went for help! I jumped the bike! I don't want you to die! Mummy, please don't die! Charlie clutched at her mother's hand. Annabel's eyes flickered open for the briefest second and her fingers closed around her daughter's blistered hand.

Chapter Four

It was two days later when their father told the impatient twins that they could at last go to visit their mother in hospital.

"Mummy is much better but we can only stay for a short time because she tires so easily," he explained to the excited girls. "And furthermore, you must not bounce about on her bed or be loud. It is a hospital after all and people need peace and quiet in order to get better."

"We won't be noisy — promise!" they yelled in unison.

George raised his eyes skywards in mock despair and bundled them into the car.

When they arrived, armed with bunches of grapes and a large bottle of Ribena, Charlie was much relieved to see that her mother, although pale faced and in a neck brace, looked a million times better than that last image of her lying ghastly and still on the stretcher.

"Poor, poor, Mummy," shouted Sam. "What have you done to yourself and what's that big thing round your neck?"

"Sam! Be quiet!" hissed her father. "Or you will have to go outside. Mummy has cracked a vertebra in her neck."

"What's a verbere?" asked Charlie quietly.

"It's a bone, stupid! Any idiot knows that!"

"Sam! This is your very last warning!" George Lawson was losing his patience. "Mummy is still very ill and doesn't need to hear you arguing."

"I'm feeling much better today though," croaked Annabel, "and it is just so lovely to see my beautiful girls." She winced painfully as her cracked ribs complained.

"Mummy also broke a rib which punctured a lung and it's your brave ride, Charlie, through the forest to get help that made all the difference," explained George. He smiled at his wife fondly and tried to dismiss the negative thoughts of what could have happened if his young daughter had indeed not made that supreme effort and overcome her fear to go and fetch help.

The visit seemed all too short as the twins had so much news to tell about their ponies. "Humphrey is fine, Mummy, because I remembered Black Beauty and I did all the right things not like that stupid Jo boy in the story."

"Well done, sweetheart. What a clever girl you are." Sam beamed with pleasure at being back in the centre of attention. Annabel then asked Charlie, "How is poor little Marshmallow?"

"Oh Mummy, Mrs Turner called Colin Peters, the vet, and we took the trailer to pick him up and it took us ages to walk him down the track and Mr Peters had to give him a big injection before he would move. He had to have loads of stitches in his leg."

"Seven actually," interjected George

"And Mr Peters says he has to stay in his box for a while and then he will be OK and I will be able to ride him again when he's better!"

"Well that's a relief," her mother smiled.

"Mummy!" asked Sam "What happened to that horrible boy on the motorbike?"

"Did you know it was Gareth, the Major's nephew?" chirped Charlie.

"Yes, I did, dear. I believe he broke his leg quite badly. Quite what he was doing on the bridle path on his motorbike, I don't know."

"Well, my dear," said George. "It looks as if now is your chance to ask him!"

Everyone turned towards the door and there, hobbling slowly down the ward on crutches, was Gareth. His right leg was encased in a pot which stuck out from under his wide-legged striped pyjamas and clutched clumsily in his left hand was a very large bunch of red roses.

There was an awkward silence as he approached the bed.

"I, er… I've, er, brought these," Gareth stammered, breaking the silence. The roses slipped out of his hand onto the crisp white sheet. No one spoke! Gareth took a deep breath and tried again. "I don't really know what to say except that I am so dreadfully sorry to have caused you so much pain. I feel so dreadful about the whole thing. I honestly didn't realise I was on a bridle path and thought I'd do a bit of off-roading… Only I never heard the horses and when I tried to brake I lost control on the bend in the muddy bit and — well, I am just so terribly sorry." His voice trailed off into the silence and he turned awkwardly to go.

"It's Gareth, isn't it?" George was the first to break the tension. "Major Bentley's nephew?"

"Yes, that's right, although I think my uncle has just about disowned me — first I wreck his favourite hunter and now this."

"So you're the one who hurt Humphrey's legs!" admonished Sam. "He's ours now, you know, and he was in the wood when you ran over Mummy. He's the horse Charlie rode to get help."

"Goodness!" Gareth looked stunned. "I had no idea. Poor Humphrey. I bet I'm not his flavour of the month. Thank goodness you rode him home so brilliantly." He beamed a fleeting grin in Charlie's direction. "Well, I certainly won't be riding my bike for a while and certainly never again on a bridle path… I can only repeat how sorry I am." He stood there awkwardly, with not a trace of his usual arrogant self. "Er, well I'd best go now get back to the ward. Goodbye." He turned to go.

"Now just a minute, young man." The command came from George. Gareth stood, head down as he had done so many times in front of his drunken father, waiting for the inevitable tirade of verbal abuse.

"You were exceedingly foolish," George continued, "to be on a bridle path with a motorbike but I'm sure you've learnt that lesson the hard way. At least you kept your head and despite being in immense pain, gave Charlie all the encouragement she needed to get on H and ride for help." Gareth could hardly believe his ears. Was this a tone of reason and forgiveness he was hearing.

"Yes! Yes! He did! I could never have done it without him and he told me not to move Mummy and to cover her with his jacket."

"Well, for that at least we must be grateful," smiled Annabel. "I think I might have been a goner if Charlie had moved me with this cracked vertebra in my neck!"

"What about your leg?" asked Sam. "Will it be OK?"

"Oh, it was a bit mangled, they had to put pins in it so I'll be on crutches for some time yet. Well, I had better go now. Goodbye."

"Goodbye," they chorused.

"If you want to come and see us at any time, we're at Cherry Tree Farm in Thornbury village. I have a great collection of old motorbikes you might like to see." Mr Lawson held out his hand and after a moment of surprised hesitation, Gareth took it.

"Thank you, sir. I would like that very much and thank you for being so… well… er… so understanding," blushing, he turned away and stomped awkwardly towards the doors.

George watched his painful exit. "There goes a young man who's had a hard lesson. Let's hope he takes it to heart. He seems a decent young lad, just a bit on the wild side." Annabel smiled a secret smile to herself.

"I can remember another young man, very similar indeed to Gareth, who rode horses very hard and zoomed all over the place, like a lunatic, on a motorbike."

"Ahmm, well," stammered George, "that was a very long time ago." The twins looked at their father in surprise.

"Gosh, Daddy, I can't imagine you on a motorbike!" Sam was amazed.

"You're way too old!" piped up Charlie.

"Hey girls, steady on — not that old and yes I suppose I was a bit wild in my youth."

"So bad that my parents were not a bit pleased when I wanted to marry you," said Annabel.

George gazed after the disappearing Gareth. "Yes, I have to say that young man reminds me so much of myself when I was his age."

"Did you have crashes on your motorbike too?" asked Sam.

"Certainly not!" he grinned "Now c'mon you two, let's go before you start delving too deeply into my terrible and sordid past!"

They all kissed Annabel goodbye. "Bye, my darlings," she said. "Take care." She watched them fondly as they progressed down the ward where, on reaching the door, all three turned to wave. Annabel raised a weak arm and waved back. Her attention then turned to the flowers on her bed. How nice of Gareth to bring me these, she mused looking at the velvet-red petals vivid against the stark white sheets. It must have taken some courage. I must ask the nurse to put them in water.

Gareth meanwhile, breathing a sigh of relief that his apology was over and had been accepted with such grace, was making his difficult way through the hospital corridors back to his ward. He was just bracing himself to negotiate some swinging double doors when they crashed open ejecting a whirlwind of black leggings and silver studs. He tottered as he was pushed off balance.

One of his crutches slid to the floor and as he felt himself falling, he grabbed a black t-shirted arm in which was clutched a bunch of yellow chrysanthemums. He ended up on the shiny hospital linoleum in a mass of long legs and yellow petals.

"Ouch!" a shrill voice yelled. "That bloody hurts!"

"Get off my broken leg, you arse!" retorted Gareth. "What do you think you're doing? You can't fly through a hospital like that! You'll kill somebody!" He looked up in disgust straight into big brown eyes which he instantly recognised.

"Jade!"

"Gareth! Oh shit!"

There was a strained silence as they tried to extricate arms, legs and flower stalks. Suddenly Jade started to giggle helplessly.

"You do look rather fetching in your stripey jim-jams!" Gareth looked down at his tatty pyjamas and felt slightly uncomfortable – not an emotion he was used to. Then he too burst into laughter.

"Let me up, you daft tart. What are you doing here?"

Jade, still giggling helplessly, managed to raise him to his feet and retrieve his crutches.

"Actually I came to bring these now dreadfully damaged flowers to Annabel. I was late, visiting time's nearly over, so I was in a rush. More to the point, what are you doing in this part of the hospital? Shouldn't you be on the orthopaedic ward? I heard about your leg. Oh my God, I am so sorry. I hope I haven't damaged it," she gabbled. "Does it hurt?"

"It didn't but it does now!" Gareth patted his pot ruefully.

"Well, you've only yourself to blame. Fancy riding your motorbike on a bridle path. How ridiculous."

"Don't you start. I've had enough grief from my parents and feel bad enough as it is."

Gareth turned to go. "And if you must know, I've just been to see Annabel to grovel in her presence and apologise profusely. I must say, she and George were pretty decent about the whole thing. All things considered."

"That's because they're lovely people. After all, you did nearly kill her."

"For goodness sake, don't you think I don't know that!" Gareth's handsome face was creased in pain. "I can't feel any more ashamed than I do now so kindly bugger off and leave me alone."

Jade, her anger abating, felt an unbidden wave of compassion for the forlorn figure before her.

"Can I help you back to your ward."

"No thanks!" Gareth was emphatic "I think I would be better off on my own."

"OK, just asking, no need to be snorpy! I've said I was sorry." Jade picked up the flattened chrysanthemums and with only moderate success tried to put them back into a semblance of a bunch. Gareth absentmindedly picked a yellow petal from the front of her t-shirt and added it to the bunch.

"Oh well, best be going," said Jade, turning away before he could see the faint flush of pink rising in her cheeks. "Seeya," and with that she rushed off down the corridor.

"Oh yeah, see ya!" Gareth watched her hasty progress and was left standing alone in the corridor feeling that a huge breath of fresh air had just suddenly enveloped him and had just as suddenly, disappeared. Normally so cool and self-controlled, he just could not put a finger on why he felt rather self-conscious and somehow bereft. Must be the pain killers he thought to himself and carried on to the TV room to watch the rugby.

Over the next couple of weeks Sam and Charlie rode out a lot together. Charlie rode Humphrey because as she explained to Sam, "After galloping all that way half hanging off and jumping Gareth and the motorbike, I feel quite safe just pottering about on a quiet hack." Their father had taken a lot of persuading but finally gave his consent as long as there was no cantering, they had a mobile phone and someone in the house was informed as to which route they were going to take.

Charlie loved riding Humphrey and when a schedule arrived one Saturday morning for the Thornbury Village Show she pleaded with her father to be allowed to take him as Marshmallow had still not yet quite recovered from his leg injury. George was not keen but after ringing Jade to seek her advice, agreed to look through the schedule with them to see if there were any suitable classes.

"Jade says, certainly not the Hunter Class because you're far too young and the judge needs to see you gallop. Not a good idea!" He ran his eyes down the page.

"Working Hunter, Local Riding Horse, Family Horse, now Jade seems to think that those last two might be a possibility along with the Tack and Turnout class."

"What can I do with Snowflake?" demanded Sam, quite put out at not being the centre of attention.

"Jade suggests that you do the Local Riding Pony class, maybe the Under-twelve equitation class and the Gymkhanas."

"Oh great!" Sam yelled. "When is it?"

"Next Saturday!"

"WHAT?" both girls shrieked in unison. "That doesn't leave us much time. We'll have to practise like mad!"

Fortunately for them, their mother was discharged from hospital the following Monday and she spent a lot of time with the girls at her bedside, explaining the different classes.

"Now Family Horse or Pony means exactly what it says. A horse or pony suitable to be ridden by any member of the family. Looks are not important but manners and suitability are. Snowflake is too small and is probably not well mannered enough!"

"But he…" began Sam indignantly.

"But nothing," Annabel was quick to interject. "Do be quiet and listen! I've spoken to Jade and she says," Sam was immediately quiet, "that Humphrey, although a bit big, is probably going to be the best bet. However, it will be good experience for both of you. Sammy, for the equitation and the ridden pony class, you must practise making Snowflake do a figure of eight in both trot and canter then canter quite fast and come back to a smooth halt without any fussing or pulling. Quite a tall order so I have arranged for Jade to come over a couple of times this week to give you lessons."

"What about Riding Horse?" asked Charlie.

"Ah well you will have to walk, trot and canter round the ring with all the others just as you will in Family Horse and Pony and then you will have to do a small show of your own or the judge will ride each horse. Then you have to run Humphrey up in hand."

"Gosh, what on earth is that?" asked Sam. "It sounds very complicated to me."

"It's actually very simple," smiled Annabel. Bring Humphrey and the pony onto the drive in front of my window and I'll shout instructions from my sick bed." The girls duly stood by their mounts' heads under the front bedroom window. Annabel told them how to stand up their horses squarely so that the judge could assess their conformation and then explained how they should walk their horses away from and then trot back to the judge in a straight line.

"Why are we doing this bit?" panted a running Sam.

"This is so the judge can see whether your animal moves straight or not. Some horses and ponies fling their legs about when they move."

Humphrey was very well behaved.

"I'm sure he's done all this before," exclaimed Charlie breathlessly as she was dragged back under the window by a swiftly trotting Humphrey.

"Yes, my dear, I'm sure he has. Snowflake, however, is a completely different kettle of fish!" Snowflake stood quietly next to Humphrey in the imaginary line of horses but would not stand straight or square for the non-existent judge and refused point blank to move when asked to walk away and trot back. Eventually after much pushing and shoving and giggling on the part of the twins and much amused advice from their mother, Snowflake was persuaded to leave his pal. With a smack on the rump and much clicking and waving of arms, he proceeded at a snail's pace up the drive. He had only gone a few metres when he whirled round and with a red-faced Sam clinging to the end of the reins, shot back in line next to Humphrey where he proceeded to rive plants out of the herbaceous border.

"I think that's enough for today and don't worry, Sammy, because H won't be in the same class as you so Snowflake will not be trying to get back to him all the time." Sam patted Snowflake's nose thoughtfully.

"It's a good job you're not always like this," she muttered. Snowflake rolled his eyes and snatched a dahlia.

Annabel settled back into her bed and listened contentedly to the clip clop of hooves as the girls led the big bay horse and the little grey pony back to the stables. How lovely it is to be home, she thought, and how lucky I am to be alive. Goodness me, I feel so much better already!

Saturday morning saw the girls up at a ridiculously early hour to feed and prepare their animals for the show. In the absence of their mother, Jade had volunteered to help and although muttering darkly about having to get up at sparrow's fart, she agreed to come over early and plait up. Sam and Charlie were extremely grateful.

Although they had both attempted to plait their ponies' manes on previous occasions, the whiskery door knobs bore no resemblance to the row of tiny neat plaits which Jade had managed to conjure out of even Marshmallow's bog brush of a mane. Jade plaited furiously and the girls brushed, washed and scrubbed until even Snowflake was a vision in white.

The girls arrived at the show in good time and Jade parked the Range Rover and trailer under a shady tree in the ever-increasing line of equine transport.

"Oh crumbs!" exclaimed Sam. "Just look at all these people. I'm beginning to get butterflies already."

"So am I," agreed her twin. "I wish I could've brought Marshmallow instead of Humphrey — he's so big. I don't think I want to do this."

"If you think I got up at silly o'clock this morning for you two to wimp out, you've another think coming!" Jade was emphatic! "Now come on, panic not — H is a sweetie, Snowflake is fab at gymkhanas and you're both very capable of doing well. Just pretend you're in the paddock at home, have a lovely time and enjoy! This is for fun remember! Just think positively and do your best. No one minds whether you win anything or not."

"Except us!" they chirped in unison. Jade laughed and remembered how competitive she was herself.

"OK, forget that last speech. Just get out there and win some rosettes!"

One hour later Charlie and Humphrey were standing a very creditable 5th in a line of twelve (a real line up this time) in the Riding Horse Class. The judge rode Humphrey and said, "Thank you, my dear," as she handed the reins back to his small jockey. "What a pleasant ride."

Charlie beamed and gave H a proud pat. When she led him out in hand she stood him up properly and made sure he wasn't resting a leg and glanced over to Jade at the side of the ring who gave her a thumbs up sign. The judge spent what seemed ages looking at Humphrey's front legs. Charlie ended up with a 6th rosette and as the judge handed it up to her she smiled.

"Well done, my dear. What a lovely horse but he's more of a hunter than a riding horse type and his legs have taken some hammering."

"I know," replied Charlie seriously. "That shit, Gareth, rode him through a bog out hunting, when he shouldn't have done"

"Ah," said the judge, managing to keep a straight face as she turned quickly to the next horse in line.

Charlie cantered H round on the lap of honour, the purple rosette fluttering from his bridle. She had a huge grin on her face and pretended she was at the Horse of the Year Show. Humphrey looked a picture, his bright bay coat gleamed in the sunlight and his ears were pricked as he listened and took in all the activity at the ringside.

The show was alive with horses, ponies and people. Flags were flapping gently in the light breeze and mobile shops were busy setting up their stalls. Tack shops, plant stalls, a cake and jam stall selling goodies made by the local WI, pottery stalls, craft stalls and a host of local produce stalls. In the produce tent old John, Major B's gardener, was found bemoaning the fact that his bunch of three prized carrots were only worthy of second place and he had been pipped at the post by Bill, his drinking buddy at The Three Shoes, who had never grown a decent vegetable in his life!

The Thornbury Brass Band, tucked under a green and white striped awning struck up the rousing Rule Britannia", which brought a smile to even the most miserable countenance and a spring in the step of everyone passing by, both young and old. Playing gustily in the front row was Tom, the farmer's son, who had helped Humphrey out of that fateful bog. Winter was spent in a different front row, playing prop in the local rugby team, but in summer he swapped his striped rugby shirt and sweatband for the gleaming brass-buttoned blue jacket and cap of the Thornbury Brass Band. Tom stood to play his solo. Passers-by stopped in amazement at the wonderful run of notes which soared so confidently from the euphonium he held in his large hands. It seemed impossible that this huge rugby player with his podgy fingers could find each tappet with such unwavering dexterity and produce music of such profound depth. Even his rugby team mates on the way to a Neanderthal booze up in the beer tent clapped and cheered at the end of his solo and Tom's face lit up with a wry grin. This was his talent. He hadn't told them yet that he had been accepted as second euphonium player in a brass band. But not any old brass band – this was the world-famous Brighouse and Rastrick Brass Band. The band he had seen at Morley Town Hall when he was a kid. The band that had transported him that day into a world of amazing music. A world into which he had dared to aspire. Now at long last this aspiration was to become a reality. Perhaps he would tell them later on this afternoon and they could drink lots of pints in celebration.

The next class for Humphrey and Charlie was the Family Horse. H behaved like an angel. During his show he stood like a rock whilst Charlie managing to dismount by sliding down his foreleg to the floor, and then had to let down her stirrup nearly to the last hole so that she could climb back up into the saddle. He cantered quite fast round the ring when asked for extended canter and for one awful moment she felt a twinge of fear as the memory of that other fateful gallop came flooding back. She tweaked the reins and whispered desperately, "Whoa, whoa, lad, whoa."

H flicked a listening ear backwards and slowed quietly down to a steady canter and trot and then halted in a perfect square in front of the judge. Charlie beamed with relief, dropped the reins, saluted the judge then leant forward, wrapped her arms around his glossy neck and gave him a fierce hug. There was a fortunate round of applause from the spectators which, thank goodness, made H prick his ears and raise his head instead of putting it down to eat the grass which had been his intention and which would have sent Charlie on a slippery slide, head first down his neck.

After Humphrey, all the other horses had to give an individual show which seemed to take forever and as George admitted was like 'watching paint dry.' (George had just arrived in his car, straight from a morning's work at the office.) The judge then seemed to take ages adding up marks with her steward. Finally, they called out. "Will number 106 come forward, please." No one stirred from the line. The steward pointed at Charlie and Humphrey who were both by now sleeping in the warm sun.

"You dear. The little girl on the big bay."

Charlie was still half asleep. "Who me?"

"Yes, dear, you. You're the winner!"

Charlie moved Humphrey forward and through a mist of tears saw her father amongst a host of spectators clapping and cheering, and caught sight of Sam and Jade leaping up and down and shrieking madly. In the members' tent adjoining the ring Major B and Lady Smythe smiled broadly as they raised their glasses of champagne in a toast to her.

Once again Humphrey cantered around the ring with a rosette fluttering from his bridle only this time the colour was the elusive red. Everyone greeted the pair as they left the ring and Humphrey was patted and kissed and given a thousand titbits. John materialised from nowhere.

"Now then, mi ole lad, I've missed you. What a great horse you are. 'Ere you might as well have these." Humphrey happily munched his way through the second prized carrots, oblivious to the sweat and toil of their production and enjoyed all the fuss and commotion which surrounded him.

Soon afterwards he was loaded into the trailer with a huge net of hay to wait until Sam and Snowflake had finished their gymkhana classes. They'd already notched up a very creditable third in the under-twelve equitation class and a fourth in tack and turnout. By the time the last gymkhana class had finished it was five o'clock and they had won a 1st in Musical Poles. This was due to the fact that Snowflake always galloped like mad towards the last pole when the music stopped and Sam had become very adept at dismounting very quickly and hanging on to his mane so that her feet barely touched the floor on the run in. They also had a second in the bending race and a fourth for walk trot and lead. Sam was thrilled to bits as she led Snowflake and the delighted entourage of family and friends towards the Range Rover and trailer in the horsebox park. What a good day it had been.

As they went through the gateway into the horsebox field, it looked rather desolate as most of the exhibitors had already gone home. They looked along the sparsely dotted horseboxes and the couple of trailers which were left and their excited chatter turned suddenly into a stunned silence.

"My God!" exclaimed George. "It's gone — Range Rover and trailer — the whole caboodle! The whole damn lot has gone!"

"But," screamed Charlie, "it can't have gone! What about Humphrey?"

"Oh no!" exclaimed Jade as she sank onto a nearby tree stump and promptly burst into tears.

Chapter Five

Humphrey travelled in the trailer for a long time. At one stage he was stationary for quite a while and a bucket full of water was offered from which he drank long and gratefully. It was at this stop that the number plates were changed. The journey continued far into the night and the trailer and horse were ferried swiftly from Holyhead across the Irish Sea to Dun Laoghaire just South of Dublin City in Southern Ireland.

Finally, after thirty-six hours of travelling the side ramp was lowered and the intelligent bay face peered out into a drizzling grey dawn. The breast bar was unhooked and H staggered stiff-legged, slowly down the ramp.

"Put the lad into the field and let him have some of the Emerald Isle's emeralds." The scrawny face bent into an ugly smile at his own joke. "D'you get the joke, Patrick? Emerald Isle — emeralds. D'you get it now?" Flynn's thick Irish brogue broke into a hoarse cackle which immediately turned into a rasping cough.

"Why don't you just shut the feck up and get the poor horse into the field. The lad has run up with all this travelling, to be sure. Just look at the state of him." Patrick, bald and short and squat, quite the opposite of his partner in crime, folded his muscular arms onto his chest and narrowing his hard eyes, cast an experienced glance over the jaded animal in front of him. H was indeed a sorry sight. He was hungry and dehydrated. He had hollows in his flanks and his coat was hard and staring. His tail was filthy and matted where he had scoured on the journey and his buttocks were raw where he had rubbed them on the back bar of the trailer as he had fought to keep his balance both on the ferry and on the twisting route of the narrow Irish country lanes.

Flynn's coughing fit subsided enough for him to straighten up his bean pole of a body and take another drag of the cigarette still dangling from his thin mean lips.

"To be sure it was a real bonus to be getting a horse into the bargain and not a bad sort of a horse neither."

Patrick gave Flynn a piercing stare.

"You! You surely have not the brains of a flea. The idea was to take an empty trailer. 'Tis only because we had a spot of luck on our side that we be getting away with it so easy."

"Oh to be sure 'twas a piece of cake, it was. There's no need to be fretting. We'll soon be able to offload this handsome beast. He just needs a bit of grass to bring him round." H was duly led to the field which was of about six acres, full of good grass and had a trickle of a stream running through the corner. He walked stiffly to the water and drank thirstily then dropped his head and tore at the grass. The two men watching leaned on the gate and chuckled.

"Well he surely is a little hungry. Let's leave him be. He'll be fine here for a while, so he will. I wonder now how much we could be getting for him?" Patrick's brain clocked into overdrive as he visualised a huge pile of unplanned euros in his grubby palm and he rubbed his hands together greedily. He had a wrinkled kindly-looking face which bore an uncanny resemblance to old John Major Bentley's gardener. However, that's where any similarity abruptly ended. For behind the kindly face and Irish charm were eyes as hard as steel and a nasty temper and character to match. Many people had been taken in by his friendly smile, only the most discerning realising that it never reached his flinty eyes. If ever a book should not have been judged by its cover then Patrick was that book.

"Come along then, Flynn. Look sharp now." He turned back to the Range Rover and trailer. "Let's take this lot to the boys to be resprayed and then we can get off home. A drop of Guinness will surely not go amiss now will it?" Flynn's mean ferret face lit up at the thought of alcohol. He lit up another cigarette, ran a grubby hand through his greasy black curls and they both piled into the Range Rover and disappeared down the bumpy track.

Humphrey ate steadily, occasionally raising his head, ears pricked, watching and listening for any sign of life, either horse or human. He whinnied a few times hoping that perhaps Snowflake or Marshmallow would answer but no other sound echoed back from the vast green swards of the surrounding hills. Humphrey was completely alone.

During the first few days after Humphrey's disastrous disappearance everyone's hopes were high that he would soon be found and returned to them. The twins rode and cycled everywhere in and around the village and put up 'Stolen' notices which their father had typed for them on the computer.

REWARD!
PLEASE HELP US FIND HUMPHREY, OUR MUCH-LOVED HORSE.
HE WAS STOLEN FROM THORNBURY VILLAGE SHOW ALONG WITH A BLUE RANGE ROVER AND TRAILER. REG – LAWS 1
BRIGHT BAY HUNTER. EIGHT YEARS OLD 16.2H H. CROOKED WHITE STRIPE. THICKENED TENDON ON NEAR FORE.

On the bottom was a heartbreakingly lovely picture of Humphrey and Charlie doing their lap of honour at the show with the red rosette flying triumphantly from H's bridle. (The very same rosette that was now hidden in the bottom of Charlie's wardrobe because every time she saw it she burst into tears.)

Please help us find him was the final plea at the very bottom of the flier written very badly by Sam.

The whole thing brought a tear to the eye of many a villager and even to some of the townie commuters, who didn't even like horses much and only lived in the country because it was fashionable.

P C Brake, tall and angular, came round for a statement.

"Well, Mr Lawson," he said, his young face wrinkled in disapproval. "If the animal in question had been chipped or freeze branded then you would have made our job much easier and we would have a far better chance of retrieving the said animal." George wondered why most policemen and especially this young lad who looked about fourteen, always spoke in formalised terms which hardly sounded part of the normal English language.

"I know I know. It was foolish of us and was always on the agenda but I'm afraid we never got round to it. Stupidly we are victims of the 'it'll never happen to us' syndrome. To be quite honest, he wondered why he felt he had to justify himself to this pimply youth. "We didn't think anyone would bother to steal a horse like H because he has had injury to his legs and wasn't worth anything."

"Except to us," said Annabel softly.

"Yes, my dear, except to us."

"That's the trouble, sir," the pimply youth would not let go. "People (he missed out the — like you) always think it can't happen to them but," he added unnecessarily, "it can and it does. We think that the thieves took the opportunity to steal your Range Rover and trailer and the horse was just an unplanned bonus. We've been having a lot of vehicle thefts in this area, particularly horseboxes and trailers. We believe there is an organised gang changing plates and shipping the vehicles abroad as soon as possible. Or they may even have stripped the said vehicle down immediately and shipped it abroad as spare parts." George blanched at the thought of his beloved Range Rover being broken down for spare parts but wisely kept silent as his wife cut in.

"The loss of the car and trailer, Mr Brake, is upsetting but they are after all only pieces of metal." George opened his mouth to speak but glancing at Annabel, closed it again firmly. "They can be replaced, whereas Humphrey..." Her voice trailed off into a miserable silence.

"Well Mr and Mrs Lawson, I can assure you that we will do our best but it is not looking too hopeful. We have informed horse sales up and down the country but as I have said, it does make our life so much more difficult if the animal is not chipped. Good day to you both and let us hope for a positive outcome." He shook their hands solemnly and strode out to his patrol car, leaving George and Annabel staring after him feeling very miserable and more than a little guilty.

The loss of Humphrey seemed to send out waves of dejection which affected everyone.

Major B put a half page 'Missing' ad in Horse and Hound and he and Jade scoured the country attending every Horse and Pony sale from Scotland down to Devon. Major B, Lady Smythe and the Lawsons had every horse and dog they owned microchipped. The twins were inconsolable, school work suffered and both parents came back from parents' evening with a stern lecture. Jade found solace in a gold hoop navel piercing, which went septic and hurt like hell. Old John's prize carrots caught some rare blight which spread to the rest of his vegetables because he forgot to spray. Consequently, his pristine vegetable patch became a tangle of dying leaves in a sad corner of the otherwise beautifully tended lawns and rose beds.

Although everyone made a supreme effort, all trace of Humphrey was gone and the image of the beautiful bay head with its crooked stripe became more of a distant memory as the weeks passed.

Three weeks after his disappearance, a disconsolate Jade was half-heartedly cleaning tack at Eagle Manor when her phone bleeped a received text. Hi you daft tart! How is everything? What are you up to? Might go to Shipley sales to moz t look 4 H. Leg still bad want t drive? G. Jade read slowly the stark black letters on the pale blue background and tried to quash the queasy churning in her stomach. O. K. she text back Will check wiv Major. She deliberated long and hard whether to finish with Luv Jade or an x or xxx but finally decided that a simple J would suffice and pressed SEND. A few moments later another text beeped through. O. K. great. C U at mine 8.30 G.

So it was that 8.30 next morning saw a rather nervous Jade grimace into a CCTV camera and watch the huge iron gates swing silently open to admit her battered old golf onto the immaculate driveway of Silverdale Towers. Jade had never been to Silverdale before and had only seen it from a distance when out hunting. Rounding the bend at the top of the drive she came face to face with the most beautiful house she had ever seen. The drive wound around a still lake upon which numerous swans floated in serene contentment. Swallows dipped and soared above the ripples and weeping willows dipped their feathery fronds into the water's edge. A soft stone terrace reached up around the house and was encased by masses of mauve clematis and pink climbing roses. Long casement windows glinted in the early sunlight and were reflected in the shimmering lake.

Suddenly the peace was shattered by a black spotted Great Dane who rose lazily from the huge arched porch , gave a million decibel bark and bounded down the steps to Jade's car. He then proceeded to launch his huge front paws onto her driver's window and stared eyeball to eyeball through the glass. The noise was deafening and great chunks of slobber sprayed from his huge teeth and ran down the glass. Jade sank as far down as her seat would allow and tried to look non- threatening. Which wasn't difficult!

"Good dog," she muttered hopelessly. "Good boy — please don't eat me. Friend?"

"Oh for Gods' sake, Watson, stop trying to look fierce. Get down you daft twit!" Gareth's dulcet tones rang out. Watson gave Jade a slobbering grin and bounced back over to the doorway where Gareth was balancing uneasily on his crutches. "Don't worry about him he's as soft as putty."

"Mmm," thought Jade as she gingerly opened the car door a fraction of an inch. Watson, ignoring Gareth's shouts to "STAY", about turned and galloped towards her once more, squeezed his huge bulk into the narrow opening, placed his lion paws on Jade's shoulders and licked her face enthusiastically. Jade collapsed into giggles of relief. "Call the brute off. I can't breathe."

"At least he likes you — you should see what he does to the visitors he doesn't like!"

"He's huge!" Jade struggled to get out of the car "He's just like that dog in *Hound of the Baskervilles*, you know the one which keeps appearing out of that foggy moor." Gareth rolled his eyes heavenward. Jade stopped. "Ah got it! Penny has dropped! Sherlock Holmes — Watson — Doctor. Right?"

"Der! Bit slow on the uptake but I suppose it proves you might be able to read or at least watch a film!"

"Don't start, you pompous twit! Both, actually! Don't you just love that gorgeous Benedict Cumberbatch in Sherlock. Just a young version of good old Basil Rathbone in all those old films. He was just so dark and brooding. Bit like myself actually! Come on, the sale starts at ten and we have quite a way to go. Shall I help you? You poor lame thing!"

"No thanks! I'm just fine but we're not going in that old heap are we?" Gareth cast a disdainful glance in the direction of the Golf.

"Yup! Afraid so! Major B's Land Rover is in for repair so it's this or nothing."

Gareth managed to shoo the still slobbering Watson into the house and hobbled painfully over to the car. He wrinkled his nose in disgust as he lowered himself gingerly into the passenger seat, pausing only to remove two empty coke cans, a tattered Horse and Hound, and a smelly brown banana skin. He had a fit of sneezing as bits of straw and disturbed dust floated casually in the footwell.

"Sorry 'bout the mess," said Jade tartly. "Haven't had time to clean it out." Gareth looked down his nose and deigned not to reply.

The drive was uneventful and rather quiet, Gareth grimacing in pain as Jade drove up the bumpy track into the sale yard.

"Sorry," she muttered. "Does it still hurt?"

"Only when you drive like a maniac over every pothole in the bloody road. Actually, it is generally feeling better. I should be having the pins removed in two weeks' time"

"Ouch!" exclaimed Jade. "Sounds pretty painful to me."

"Yes — well it was my own stupid fault. How's Mrs Lawson doing?"

"Oh, much better thanks but the whole family's devastated over H being stolen. I mean — no one has horses stolen from around these parts. Why oh why was poor old H in the wrong place at the wrong time?"

"Well let's do something positive and start looking for him here." Jade helped Gareth out of the car and gave him his crutches.

"Right! Into battle! Let's go!"

Jade and Gareth scoured the sale for two hours checking every lot and every stable. They gave the 'Horse Stolen' fliers to everyone who would take one. Gareth approached everybody, asking in his cut glass accent. "I say, has anyone seen this horse about. There's a huge reward for his recovery you know!"

"'Ow much, lad?" asked one weather-beaten old farmer.

"Well, I actually don't know exactly but it will be very substantial!"

"I'll keep a right good look out. I get abowt a bit, tha knows."

Gareth looked at the wrinkled red face and the missing front tooth and thought that 'getting abowt a bit' probably meant a weekly trip to the village pub and that he couldn't have been out of the Yorkshire Dales in seventy-five years.

"Me an' t missus, we went to that there Australia, tha knows, last year. I've allus wanted to go there. Me son lives there now. Ee, we 'ad a grand time. That ther Sydney opera 'ouse with them sails ont' roof it were amazing. Aye, 'n' me and missus we 'ad a ride on camels at a cattle station in't outback on't way t' Alice Springs and that there Ayres Rock it's a magnificent sight at sunset. You can see why them aboriginals thought it were sacred like. I do 'ope you find yer 'oss lad its 'orrible when y 'ave animals and you don't know what's 'appened to 'em, like. I'm off now to look for a nice, young 'oss for me other son to qualify this season. We love us point-to-pointing in't spring. Keeps us goin' thro't winter 'til our next trip. We're off on one of them there world cruises next." With that, he bustled off leaving Gareth standing in a state of shock!

"Close your mouth, Gareth!" Jade giggled. "That there is Bobby Miles. He owns half of Yorkshire and is a great old boy. He's big mates with my aunt. Have you ever been to Australia?" she asked sweetly.

"Er. no actually. Well I'll be blowed," he muttered. "Who would 'ave- oops — have thought…"

"Always be careful what you say to folks around here," Jade admonished. "One never quite knows to whom one may be speaking! Remember what good old Rudyard said."

"Eh?"

"If you can talk with crowds and keep your virtue, or walk with Kings — nor lose the common touch."

"Bloody hell," thought Gareth, "today is full of surprises!"

By the end of two hours they were tired and dejected. Once their hopes were raised when they spied a bright bay head in a row of loose boxes. Jade rushed down only to find that the bay face, though attractive enough, sported a big white blaze instead of the crooked stripe she had hoped for. Jade stood and wept miserably then felt a strong comforting arm around her shoulders.

"Come on, old thing, let's go home. Maybe we could stop at The Highwayman on the way and have a quick drink."

This they duly did but their spirits were not raised by a shot of alcohol nor by the fact that Jade's boyfriend, Dan, was in the snug, very drunk and snogging a very pretty blonde girl who looked like a younger version of Louisa Langley- Fox.

"Davina! What are you doing? Aren't you supposed to be in school?" asked Gareth briskly.

"No. Hi Gareth, shweetie. No problem cosh I have been shent home ill."

"Obviously not ill enough." Jade flushed crimson, turned on her heel and stormed out, closely followed by a hobbling Gareth. Dan was conspicuous by his absence.

"What a shit!" exclaimed Jade. "And he told me he was working! I wonder how long that's been going on."

"Quite a while by all accounts," said Gareth and then looked at Jade's stricken face and wished he had kept quiet.

"Why didn't you tell me?" she howled.

"Didn't think it was any of my business. If it makes you feel any better, her sister did just about the same to me — only worse," he added darkly. "And in my house and with one of my so-called friends. It must be a genetic thing!" For some reason Jade felt immediately a little better and gazed up at Gareth in amazement.

"Gosh, what did you do?"

"Pretty much the same as you but not as ladylike! I hurled a lot of abuse and I think a very precious vase of my mother's. She still thinks Watson knocked it off the shelf! He's a great alibi, Watson. He can never drop one in the shit!"

Jade managed a faint smile. "Hey ho! He was a bit of a plonker anyway. I think we'd already come very near to the end of the road but it's a bit of a pride thing. I wanted to be the one to finish it!!"

"He'll be grovelling tomorrow when he's sobered up. And then what will you do?"

"Oh — take him back probably!"

"Why?"

"Good question, dunno really. Maybe anyone is better than no one."

They drove back to Silverdale in companionable silence. On arrival Jade helped Gareth out of the car and onto his crutches.

"Would you like to come in for a coffee?" he asked.

"No thanks. I'm afraid I'm lousy company at the moment — but I'll get over it!"

Gareth gently moved a stray wisp of hair away from her eyes.

"Jade, you daft tart. Don't you dare be a victim. You are worth so much more than some drunken twit. You're quite pretty you know in a weird sort of way and do have the most amazing eyes. They're like deep pools to drown in." Jade looked up in surprise waiting for the joke punchline but it never came. Instead Gareth stared a bright blue stare that seemed to melt some icy shard in her soul and very gently touched his lips on hers. "I'll ring you!"

Chapter Six

After ten days of sunshine and good grass H felt more like his old self. The hollows in his flanks had filled out and his coat, although dirty, had a healthy sheen to it. One early morning when the sun was just rising above the surrounding hills and casting faint dappled glows across the valley, Patrick and Flynn clambered out of a battered pickup and leaned on the gate. Humphrey, short of company both equine and human, trotted over to investigate, arched his neck and blew loudly down his nostrils.

"He surely looks well, the horse, this morning." Flynn sucked in hard on his dangling cigarette and went into his usual paroxysm of coughing.

"'Tis time you gave up that terrible weed," warned Patrick. "To be sure you have a cough and a half there. Can you not stop coughing for a moment. 'Tis getting on my nerves, so it is. 'Tis time we got this fine horse on his way now. Let's be getting a few coins in our pockets for all our time and trouble."

With that they both turned away, climbed into the truck and disappeared up the lane in a cloud of dust and exhaust fumes.

When the sun had reached its zenith and the faint dapples had transformed into deep dancing shadows across the green hills, the two men reappeared. This time it wasn't the battered old truck, but an equally ancient horsebox which spluttered and bounced its way to the gateway. Humphrey raised his head in mid-munch, spun round, galloped to the far end of the six acres and resumed grazing. Patrick swore loudly and set off across the field. H turned to face the two men as they huffed and puffed towards him, the long stick-like frame of Flynn lagging behind, as unused to any form of exercise, he tried to draw in more oxygen though his smoke-damaged lungs.

"Hurry up will you, now. You're like an old man, y'are!" Patrick's short muscular legs propelled him forward at a brisker pace. H could see the halter rope behind his back. "Whoa there, my lad. Come on then, my old son, let's be having you." Patrick spoke to him softly in a soothing Irish brogue. Humphrey watched him warily then just as he reached out to touch his neck he whirled round, leapt off all fours and galloped pell-mell, squealing and bucking, to the other end of the field. Humphrey was enjoying himself. This process was repeated three times, the two men were getting redder and redder and Patrick's soothing Irish brogue had ascended into a torrent of shrill obscenities. Finally, the two men stomped off down the field, Patrick hurling the halter in H's direction as he went. H once more settled down peacefully to graze. However, his peace was short lived. Late in the afternoon the horsebox reappeared but this time it was followed by the pickup truck. Patrick had brought reinforcements!

H watched Patrick and Flynn alight from the horsebox followed by another three men from the pickup.

He walked quietly over to the gate and stood patiently whilst Patrick slipped a halter over his ears.

"Well I'll be..." exclaimed Patrick giving H a sharp slap with the halter rope out of sheer frustration. H shot backwards and rolled the whites of his eyes. The other three men muttered and grumbled. The tallest one turned to the others. "C'mon boys, let's go. Fancy dragging us all this way. I thought you said the horse was a pig to catch! You owe us one Patrick!"

"Can't understand it!" replied Flynn. "He gave us a right run around this morning and that's for sure. I reckon the blighter knows when he's beat. Is that not right, Patrick?"

Patrick grunted. "Come on, let's just get the little fecker loaded!"

Humphrey nuzzled in Patrick's pocket hoping for a titbit and got a sharp smack on the nose instead.

He was duly loaded up the rickety ramp into the box to begin yet another journey into the unknown. This particular journey was, however, a fairly short one. Probably a very good job as the old wagon creaked and groaned over every bump in the road and the engine complained loudly every time it had to climb a hill. Throughout the journey in the dilapidated cab, Patrick and Flynn were deep in conversation.

"Would you not think that this fine horse will be fetching a fair price if we smarten him up and take him to the Drumalee sales next week?" enquired Flynn.

"Well now, I'm thinking we could be getting more money for the beast if we spread the word around. Mr Collins, I have word, is looking for a horse to ride up to the gallops with those fine race horses that he has, over in England."

"Ah, but you must not be forgetting that this horse does not have any sort of papers with it and Mr Collins just might be wondering where the likes of us would be getting a horse the likes of him."

"Ach, 'tis no risk at all," disagreed Patrick "We'll just tell Mr Collins that we bought the horse from up north from a farmer friend of ours who gave up hunting. We'll give him the number of one of our boys in Belfast if he wants to check." On that note, greed overcame caution and they agreed to contact him that very day. The rest of the journey passed in taciturn silence broken only by Flynn's intermittent rasping coughs.

Humphrey, at his journey's end, was unloaded and put into a small ramshackle stable which looked out onto an equally ramshackle cottage and yard. Patrick and Flynn were into the scrap metal business and evidence of their trade was everywhere. Rusty piles of metal randomly scattered, bedsteads, oil drums, springs, rusty shells of cars, twisted shapes of black and rust piled high to the sky along with old sinks, baths, machinery of all kinds and a huge mountain of old tyres. Amidst this shambles of iron and rust, H was tied to an old plough. His mane and tail were pulled and he was washed and groomed until he shone. Then he was fed and watered and settled back into his 'shack' for the night.

The next morning a silver-grey Jaguar slid gingerly into the yard and came to a halt nestling snugly between the rusting shell of an old ford van and the mountain of rubber tyres. An elegantly clad figure in a beautifully fitted Armani suit descended from the car. His £700 Cartier sunglasses shifted slightly as he perused his surroundings with ice-grey eyes and he wrinkled his nose in disgust. Not because of the scrap, for Stephen Collins had been brought up surrounded by his father's demolition and scrap metal business but because of the sheer mess and chaos of the place.

"Top o' the morning to you, sir!" greeted Patrick. "'Tis a very fine morning, is it not?"

"Good morning. Now let's get down to business." Stephen was clipped in his reply. "I am very short of time this morning. I'm flying back to England this afternoon. Where is this horse you were so adamant I should come and look at? I do hope I am not here on some wild goose chase. His smooth accent, perfected after years of practice, contrasted strangely to Patrick's Irish lilt.

"Why to be sure, here he is. Lead the fine horse out for the gentleman, Flynn my boy." Flynn dutifully led Humphrey out of the stable and stood him up in front of Stephen. Amidst the dust and debris of the yard and all its orange mountains of scrap, Humphrey looked magnificent, rather like a priceless Ming vase in the middle of a junk shop. Stephen took in his quality and breeding at a glance and ran a practiced hand down his thickened foreleg.

"Just trot him up for me please."

Patrick walked H down, weaving between the rusting wreckage and trotted him back.

H, feeling good, arched his neck, pranced around a sharp-edged harrow and bounced back towards them as sound as a pound.

"What price do you want for him?"

"Well, sir, to be sure, 'tis a splendid horse that you see before you. He's hunted with the best packs in Ireland, so he has. You'll have to be travelling a long way to be finding a horse to carry you like this lad here. He has the manners of a saint, so he has, and is as gentle as a baby. In fact, 'tis your wee daughter, is it not Flynn, who has been riding the horse out for us these last two weeks?" Flynn nodded wisely even though he didn't even have a daughter.

Stephen ran his hand through his thick silver-grey hair in frustration and fixed Patrick with his steely grey eyes. "I repeat. What price do you want for him?"

"Six thousand euros and tis surely giving him away tis at that price."

Stephen laughed loudly. That was roughly £5,300 by his reckoning. He turned on his heel and strode back towards his gleaming car. As he reached the door he cast a glance back over his shoulder. "I'll tell you what. I like the horse, I'll give you 2000 euros right now in cash to take him off your hands. No doubt you require a quick sale and your daughter will not be too upset."

"But..." stammered Flynn. "We couldn't possibly be selling this beautiful beast for that price. 'Tis daylight robbery, so 'tis." Patrick gave Flynn a thunderous look.

"And I am quite sure you gentlemen would know all about that! It is my only and final offer. Good day, gentlemen." He got into his car and reversed it silently out of the yard, leaving Patrick and Flynn shaking their heads in disbelief.

"'Tis your entire fault, to be sure!" A furious Flynn rounded uncharacteristically on Patrick. "If you hadn't asked the man for such a large sum in the first place the beast would be off our hands." His anger brought on a coughing fit.

"Maybe," relied Patrick calmly. "But you know 'tis a feeling I have that Mr Collins has his suspicions and perhaps 'tis as well he did not take the horse. Now let's be taking him to the sales next week as planned. To be sure, there's nothing lost now but the sooner the lad is gone from here the better. I would see to that cough of yours, Flynn lad, if I were you, for 'tis to be putting you in an early grave, so 'tis."

So it transpired that Humphrey found himself a few days later at the Drumalee Sales which were held on the racecourse just out of the town. The actual ring was in a domed building with sawdust spread on the circular floor and tiers of wooden seating all around. This particular sale was not for racehorses and thoroughbred youngstock but for the lowly end of the scale, hunters and riding horses and ponies and was held twice yearly. The place was seething with horses and people and the car park was full of horseboxes and trailers of every shape and size. Some of them made even the rickety old horsebox of Patrick's look rather splendid.

Each animal to be sold had a stable allocated where prospective buyers could view the animal before it went into the ring. H was number 39 and catalogued under the name of 'Red Conker', (chosen in a rare moment of inspiration by Flynn), and was not due in the sale ring until mid-morning. Patrick had brought some old tack and spent most of the morning riding H around in the exercise area where buyers gathered to watch the horses they fancied. H was quite spooky with the busy hustle and bustle which surrounded him. Horses and ponies were being ridden in all directions or being trotted up in hand in front of prospective buyers clustered round in excited groups. He shied a bit at first and was very much on his toes, expecting hounds to appear at any moment and a good day's hunting ahead. However, he was to be disappointed and soon settled down when he realised that all the horses milling around never seemed to go anywhere except in circles. There was a lot of shaking of heads and hands and slapping of palms as many deals were done before the animals got into the sale ring. Quite a lot of people showed an interest in the handsome big bay but many of them tut tutted and shook their heads when they saw his thickened tendon. One old lady, however, with a stern wrinkled face and grey hair scraped back into a neat bun asked for H to be trotted up and for him to jump the telegraph pole which had been provided for a practice fence. H cleared the fence with ease, bucking on landing, pleased to be jumping again. He trotted back to the lady who gave him a brisk pat and went over his legs thoroughly whilst Patrick babbled incessantly in her ear about the horse being the best hunter Ireland had ever seen.

"Will ye just keep quiet young man for a moment," she demanded in a voice matching her sharp green eyes. "I cannot hear myself think. What sort of a price will you be wanting for this damaged old boy?"

“Well, we have a reserve on him of 4000 euros,” lied Patrick glibly.

“Far too expensive!” retorted the lady. “I’ll give you 1500 euros for him now in cash and that is my only and final offer.” As she spoke she began to unfurl 50 euro notes from a wad of cash in her hand. This simple action was just too much for Patrick and Flynn.

“Done! cried Patrick “But to be sure, you’re getting yourself a real bargain for tis a grand horse that you’re buying here for such a paltry sum, so it is.”

“Then ’tis a deal young man,” and her bony hand grasped Patrick’s with a firm grasp which belied her frail body and shook it vigorously.

So it was that Red Conker was sold without ever reaching the sale ring which was a great pity because up there on the tiered wooden seats was Stephen Collins, resplendent in his navy Armani suit, waiting to bid for him.

The lady of the grey hair and green eyes was a Miss Sandra Sinclair. She owned a riding school and was a horse dealer. Later that evening Humphrey found himself one of many in a large yard which was full of horses and ponies of every size and shape. Every available building housed some sort of equine, from a big barn which had several loose boxes inside it, to a row of converted pig sties in which numerous small ponies were kept. Miss Sinclair had an army of girls who would appear every day, some before and some after school to muck out, turn out and exercise. The yard was very well known and well run under Sandra’s eagle eye and was very busy with much coming and going as clients came for lessons or to hire out a horse or to look for a suitable purchase. H found that he was well treated and well fed but that he had to work very hard indeed. He was often out for three hours in the morning and then another hour or two in the afternoon. Because he was willing and sensible he was extremely popular with young and old alike and the last person to ride at the end of the day expected him to be just as willing as the first. Gradually H, throughout the winter settled down to the daily toil of plodding around the arena or shuffling down the road following the horse in front with his nose next to its tail and too weary to take any interest in his surroundings. He had to suffer all types of riders, from the very nervous who clung onto his reins and were content to walk to the confident know–it–alls who wanted to gallop everywhere, using whip and spurs without any consideration for their mount. Miss Sinclair did her best to make sure that her animals were not abused but quite often the young girls in charge of hacking out were far too young to exercise any form of control over the older teenagers and adults.

There was a particular client who rode Humphrey occasionally, and whose appearance in the yard caused quite a stir. He arrived, with a mane of long brown curls framing a coarse suntanned face, in a differing array of beautiful sports cars, his favourite being a red Lamborghini. He invariably had a striking looking blond on his arm, his favourite being a willowy beauty with a skin like porcelain, full botoxed lips and always dressed in immaculately tailored riding clothes. They waited in a cloud of expensive aftershave and perfume whilst the girls all ran round smiling and fawning and tripping over themselves in the rush to get two horses ready. Even Miss Sinclair seemed slightly overawed by their appearance. Her stern face would momentarily soften and she would check herself that the horses were correctly tacked up and that their hooves were oiled and their coats gleaming.

Sometimes the slinky blonde lady rode Humphrey; she was light as a feather and had very kind hands. More often than not though it was the bronzed thickset man who swung himself into the saddle. He always settled with a heavy thump and with a cut of his whip and a dig of his spurs, would canter out of the yard and up the tarmac lane. Sandra would cringe, close her eyes and count to ten, reminding herself forcefully that this man was indeed Jack Flash (real name Dwayne Dibbling), the famous rock star, who when he visited his huge house in Southern Ireland, was one of her best customers and who she hoped would buy one of her horses for a vast sum. So business being business, she shook her head and muttered under her breath but never said a word.

It was H's undoing that he was so obliging for despite the needless use of whip and spur, having a generous nature, he did his best to please his thoughtless rider. For some reason, partly through ignorance, partly selfishness and partly showing off to the gawping girls, Jack treated H as a machine and in fact showed more consideration to his fleet of shiny cars than he did to his mount. He would never have dreamed of going uphill in the wrong gear or scrunching the gear box or driving with the hand brake still on, but he did the equivalent of all these things when he was riding Humphrey. He would gallop up all the hills no matter how long or steep or how out of breath H became. He was heavy handed on the rein, hauling the bit through H's mouth when the lightest of touches would have sufficed and kicking him on with the spurs whilst still hanging on with too tight a rein. H found with all this ignorant interference he could not balance himself properly. He would come back into the yard with flanks heaving and in a muck sweat. On one such occasion H arrived back in a state worse than usual. He was covered in white sweat and his mouth was raw and bleeding. This was too much even for Sandra's careful business mind and she strode over to Jack with a face like thunder.

"Ah Miss Sinclair," he said, before she even had chance to open her mouth to speak. "I've had a really good thrash round the woods today. I think the 'orse needs a few more oats though to keep up the pace, don't you luv?" He looked towards red lips who giggled nervously.

"Well, I've never in all my life seen…" Sandra's tirade was cut short.

"I'd like to buy this 'orse, so name your price. He can come over to my pad in England and I'll soon 'ave 'im full of oats and raring to go." His choice of words was to prove prophetic and closer to the truth than he knew. Sandra had a momentary blip as she imagined the sort of life in store for the generous-hearted bay but it was just a blip and only momentary. She choked back the rage and twisted her wrinkles into the vestige of a smile.

"Well that will be marvellous, Mr Flash. I think 10,000 euros is a fair figure. He has a marvellous temperament and will go all day for you." (Sandra was too much of a business woman to mention the bowed tendon.)

"Deal done!" exclaimed Jack. "Charlene, go get the cheque book out of the car, luv." Red lips sashayed over to the car with Jack leering at every swinging step. "Phew, she's got a great arse on 'er, that one!" Sandra's mouth set disdainfully into a prim line.

"Here you are." Jack signed the cheque with a flourish. "I've added another grand on that. 'Ave 'im shipped over to my pad next week." He flung the rein to a waiting girl, and without as much as a goodbye they sauntered back to the car, Charlene giggling as he groped her 'great arse' all the way.

Sandra was thoughtful as she untacked H herself and bathed his sore mouth with salt water.

"Well son, I'm sorry to see you go to the likes of him, for 'tis a sweet horse you are, to be sure. Far too good for him but I'm afraid 11,000 is far too much money for me to turn down. It'll keep me going for quite a while, so it will." She gave H a sugar lump and he nuzzled the calloused wrinkled hand looking for more. Miss Sinclair felt a lump rise up in her throat. "If only folks had a little more thought for others, animals and humans alike, it would surely be a much pleasanter place to live in. Eh, Conker my lad?" She stroked his nose gently. "I'm sorry, old man, but then I'm sure they will be looking after you well and perhaps you won't have to work as hard as you do here and that's for sure." As she spoke a single tear welled up in her eye and wound its way down her aged cheek. The last time Miss Sinclair had shed a tear was fifty years ago when her fiancé had been killed when combining straw on his farm. She allowed herself one deep sigh as the memories of that dreadful day came flooding back. Then she straightened her frail body, took a deep breath, wiped the tear away impatiently with the back of her hand and shook her head. "Now, Sandra girl, get a grip. 'Tis no good getting sentimental over one particular horse. Tis no way to run a business and tis no good getting attached to any of them or worrying where they will end up. You look after them whilst they're here, they're well fed and that's all you can do. 'Tis the hard head on your shoulders that has kept you going all these years, so it is." With that, she gave Humphrey's neck a brisk slap and was gone.

She didn't have the heart to watch him leave the yard the following Monday, but busied herself in the tiny kitchen absentmindedly washing dishes that were already clean. She peered through the net curtains as the girls drove the horsebox out of the yard to catch the ferry and couldn't shake off the feeling of gloom that descended on her for the rest of the day. Even banking the cheque did nothing to lift her spirits and she felt as if something good and bright and trusting had stepped out of her life; sold down the road for 30 shekels of silver.

Chapter Seven

Jack Flash lived at Flashlands (formerly Bright Acre Hall), a magnificent country mansion fronted by terraced lawns reaching down to a large lake. This glorious dwelling came with all the accoutrements that shedloads of money can buy. Swimming pools — indoor and outdoor — sauna, jacuzzis (three), gym, rarely used, tennis courts, croquet lawn — often used, surprisingly, by drunken revellers, recording studio — very often used by the same, all intertwined via walkways, surface, aerial and subterranean to make up the huge complex that was Jack Flash at home.

Internally the rooms were an eclectic mix of Jack's ever-changing taste and moods. A strange mixture of modern minimalism and sumptuous décor. So travelling from room to room could be something of a roller coaster in terms of aesthetic highs and lows. The kitchen, for instance, was a space age, futuristic, stainless steel and marble mausoleum with every conceivable electrical gadget known to man. The magnificent hallway and grand staircase, however, were a profusion of gold carpet, gold flocked wallpaper, and tacky fluffy white rugs.

A huge 1960's silver juke box nestled under the flat sword held aloft by a rigid rusting arm of a full suit of armour. This splendid knight, nicknamed Sir Moron, by gay Simon, Jack's butler, was usually draped in various items of clothing depending on the bawdiness of the previous night's party. The best yet, to Simon's mind, was Jack's fortieth spring birthday bash a few weeks ago which entertained all the beautiful — and not so beautiful — people from the music industry. This 'little party' lasted four days and thoroughly investigated all areas of sex, drugs and rock and roll. Sir Moron wore a variety of adornments over the four days but the piece de resistance for Simon was the very large genitalia made from balloons strapped to Sir Moron and supporting a full-size blow-up doll whose feet were wrapped snugly around the knight's neck. Simon chose not to disturb this dubious sculpture, knowing full well that the vicar was arriving that very morning to thank Jack personally for his generous contribution to the restoration of the church roof. The vicar on entering the hall turned a deaf ear to the sniggering staff and indeed, pausing briefly at the knight and the doll in flagrante before him, said, "Ah, another party I see. Was Elton John in attendance? I do so like his music." He then swept, cool as a cucumber, into the drawing room to wait for Jack. The vicar's street cred went up by at least ten notches and Simon, for a nanosecond, even considered going to church.

Humphrey, now known as Conker, had a very comfortable loose box in an immaculate square of a stable yard. The other stables had been converted into garages for Jack's considerable fleet of cars. H was neighbour to a large silver Rolls Royce, two BMWs, a Maserati and, of course, the Lamborghini. Buying Conker was Jack's latest craze. He had earned so much money from his latest album that had topped the charts and stayed there for four weeks that he had almost run out of things to spend it on. He had tried hang gliding, hot air ballooning, micro lighting, flying lessons — not too successful because it involved a twenty-four-hour abstinence from 'bottle to throttle', racing cars and bikes, skiing, water and snow, sailing, and polo — not too successful because he kept falling off. Jack now decided that he should settle down, spend more time at home and have a horse to ride.

Humphrey was looked after by Jack's chauffeur come bodyguard, who unlike the gorgeous Kevin Costner was a great shaven thug with arms emblazoned with tattoos and biceps the size and consistency of rocks. This was Brian, surly and monosyllabic; he looked after H unwillingly and with the minimum of effort. "Bleedin' 'orse," he would chunter with his East End twang. "Who does 'e bleedin' think I am, bleedin' John Wayne?"

The first few weeks were, however, reasonable enough and Jack rode whenever he could which was most days. He bought a set of show jumps and set them up in the small paddock. H was quite happy to pop round them, despite Jack hanging on to his teeth and banging about on his back.

All went well until the third week after H's arrival. Brian had come to untack the horse after Jack had been out for a morning ride but had then been called away by Jack to inspect his new low profiles on the Lamborghini. H was forgotten and left tied up in his stable for three hours. Consequently, when he was finally led to the field, he danced around and tossed his head impatiently. Brian, former bricklayer and long-standing friend of Jack's ever since they had worked together on the building site fifteen years ago, big bruiser that he was, actually was quite frightened of horses. This was because of their sheer size and because having dealt with dodgy people and dodgy cars for most of his life, he was not used to horses or indeed any animals and knew nothing about their behaviour.

"Come 'ere, you bleedin' thing," he shouted, giving credence to the philosophy that where knowledge ends aggression begins. He yanked H's lead rope and shouted louder. "You bleedin' great brute, come 'ere!" H threw up his head in alarm, and broke into a canter. Brian hung on grimly but as H surged forward and gathered speed, brute force and ignorance were no match for three quarters of a ton of horse, and the rope slid through Brian's great shovel hand and H was away. He galloped out of the yard and straight across the terraced lawns, jumping the small bank of ornate walls on his way down to the lake. "Bugger! Bugger! Bugger! You pillocking brute." Brian gave chase.

H, fed up with being cooped up in his box and feeling the effects of extra oats which Jack true to his word had ordered to be fed to him to 'liven him up', galloped round and round the velvet lawns with Brian in red-faced pursuit. Soon the immaculate velvet turf was criss-crossed with hoof marks and flung divots and resembled a polo field after the last chukka. However, on this occasion there were no champagne clutching giggling spectators to press in divots and redress the balance, but just a seething Brian who stomped in a few clods inadvertently as he trudged towards the lake. Humphrey had a marvellous time. He would wait until Brian was within an inch of touching the dangling halter rope and would then whirl away, snorting and kicking with Brian screaming a stream of profanities, lumbering after him.

In the middle of the top lawn was a very ornate, very over the top fountain specially imported from Italy at Jack's request. The water sprayed out of the mouth of a very gaudy gilded dolphin held aloft by gold cherubs, and cascaded down a series of waterfalls into a circular pond. Mrs Beans, the housekeeper, emerged from the house to see what all the racket was about. Assessing the situation at a glance and fearing that Brian would have a heart attack if he carried on much longer, she retreated to the stables and came back with a bucket of pony nuts.

"Try these," she suggested sweetly.

H was grazing quietly close to the fountain as Brian approached him, furiously rattling the nuts in the bucket.

"Come 'ere you bleedin' great pillocking lump of 'orse flesh," he cooed. "Come to Brian." H looked up at him warily as he approached. The rattling of the nuts was too tempting and H stretched out his neck towards the bucket. Brian made a grab for the rope but H, startled by the sudden movement, whipped round and knocked Brian straight off his feet and backwards into the fountain. Brian sat amid the water lilies with the water cascading over his shaven head like some grotesque gargoyle. It was at that precise moment that Jack returned from his recording studio with Charlene on his arm. He took one look at the apoplectic Brian and burst into gales of laughter.

“Charlene darling, we seem to ’ave a mermaid in our fountain and a bleedin’ large one at that! It’s a funny colour though. I’d prefer it in bronze!”

He peered into Brian’s streaming face. “You’d ’ave thought they’d ’ave made it a bit more cheerful looking, like! I think I’ll send it back and ’ave its face redone.” He collapsed in a crumpled heap on the wrecked grass and howled with laughter. Brian picked himself up and with as much dignity as he could muster, heaved his huge bulk over the edge of the fountain and sloshed his way towards the house. “Bleedin’ ’orse! Can’t stand the bleeders!”

Charlene had laughed so much she cried and dabbing her eyes with a tissue, she walked over to H, gave him a sugar lump, patted his nose and led him to his field. Humphrey liked Charlene and walked quietly beside her, looking forward to more sugar lumps.

The outcome of this episode was that a team of gardeners spent a week repairing the lawns. Mrs Beans’ daughter, Jenny, came up from the village every day to look after Humphrey, Brian having declared emphatically that he was ‘never going near that bugger again!’ and Jack’s next single, which got to number one and stayed there for eight weeks, was called ‘Mermaid in the Fountain’.

For the next few weeks life at Flashlands was pretty good and fairly uneventful. This was mainly due to the fact that Jack was not often at home as he spent most of his time sky diving which was his latest obsession. Jack rarely rode, Jenny and Humphrey got along famously and H spent most of his days idling in the field and becoming fat and lazy. Charlene came and rode occasionally but the frequency of her visits dwindled as Jack spent more and more time freefalling with Lucy, his sky diving instructress. It seemed as if this lazy life would go on forever and indeed perhaps it would have if Jack hadn't decided to have yet another of his legendary parties.

Everything that Jack did was very much over the top as befitting his rock star image, and his parties were no exception. H galloped about his paddock and snorted in terror as a great marquee was erected on the top terraced lawn in front of the house. This was no common or garden white marquee but was an edifice of gargantuan proportions sporting gaudy wide black and silver stripes. From every pole and every corner hung great black pennants emblazoned with Jack Flash in gold lettering. They sparkled and danced as the wind caught them and on the night of the party, were lit by multicoloured computerised flashing lights which were set up all around the lawns and which pulsed in time to Jack's music.

Inside the marquee the roof was covered in swathes and ruches of black satin in which hundreds of tiny star lights twinkled and shone on the dance floor below. A great yellow inflatable whale wallowed in the clear blue water of the swimming pool and the three outdoor jacuzzis were strewn with rose petals and surrounded by twinkling night lights.

Gardeners arrived with vanloads of huge potted palms, flower displays, trees in black and silver tubs and armfuls of beautiful white lilies. They were closely followed by the caterers in their fleet of vans. Crate after crate of Bollinger, Moet, beer and wine were deposited into the house and marquee. The drinks were followed by great silver platters of caviar, king prawns, lobster, salmon and exotic fruits. Finally, there were several cases of beef burgers and sacks of frozen chips. Jack was very partial to beef burger and chips and expected his guests to be the same. Lots of people, particularly those who had been to one of Jack's parties before, and had different culinary tastes, came with their car boots stacked with various provisions, knowing that the party could last for days.

Thank goodness the party night was clear and fine and the banners sparkled their glorious best under an inky sky. Later, even the universe endorsed the celebrations by bedecking the dark night with a host of its own stars along with a silver sliver of new moon.

The guests arrived in a variety of vehicles, some in silver shadow Rolls Royce's, stretch limos and smooth sports cars. On the other hand, just as many arrived in battered old vans, motorbikes and old kit cars. It must be said that although Jack had risen to the dizzy heights of stardom and had most of the faults that more money than sense can bestow, he was very loyal to his old friends. Many of them were his former mates from the building sites in their tatty jeans and trainers, swilling beers out of cans and mingling quite happily with the champagne-quaffing, black tie and designer frock brigade. They would embellish tales of sordid lifestyles and desperate upbringings in squalid surroundings when Jack knew full well that they came from good parents and comfortable semis and in fact earned more money as plumbers and tilers and property developers than a lot of the other designer-labelled guests.

Jack Flash made his grand entrance at 9 o' clock just before the early summer light faded. Resplendent in a skin-tight black and gold shiny suit, he sky-dived from 16,000 feet with red smoke canisters on his heels and in a blaze of light. Unfortunately, he landed slightly off target in a very prickly rose bed around by the garages. Nonetheless he received an ecstatic reception as he surfaced from beneath the folds of his parachute, pulling thorns from his legs and with a big yellow rose lodged in his hair.

After that the evening progressed as one might expect. The champagne, beer and wine crates emptied very quickly, the guests became merrier, the conversation bawdier, the music louder and the state of undress scantier. The number of naked people sitting on the yellow whale became quite ridiculous and it threatened to sink at any moment. It was at this stage that Jack, rather the worse for champagne and a few lines of coke and therefore in a state of deluded expertise, decided to show off his equestrian prowess. Lurching over to the paddock and egged on by some of his equally mentally desensitized friends, he managed to find the halter on the paddock gate and fitted it upside down around Humphrey's patient head. Standing uncertainly on one of the palm pots, he managed to scramble up onto H's back and guide him through the drunken guests towards the marquee.

From then on, the rot set in. Just as they passed one of the megawatt speakers, the opening chords of 'Mermaid in The Fountain' boomed out at full volume. Up until that moment H had just managed to keep calm through all the flashing lights and raucous noise but this was the last straw. He shied violently sideways, half reared and deposited Jack in a tub of hydrangeas. Jack, whose ego was still smarting from his argument with the rose bushes, was not pleased, especially as his guests were falling about with laughter. “Yo, ride him cowboy! Ye ha!” they chorused.

Not to be outdone and with the help of willing drunken hands, Jack clambered onto Humphrey a second time. Only Charlene, not as drunk as the others because she had spent two hours in the loo crying over the increasing loss of Jack in her life, seemed concerned.

“Please don’t do this, Jack,” she whispered in his ear. “Get off the horse and let me put him away. You’re not in any fit state to ride. Please Jack,” she implored.

Jack seemed not to hear. He brushed her aside with a “Go away, you daft cow,” and with a great “YEE HA!” he kicked H into a canter and headed for a long trestle table which had been erected at the side of the marquee and on which resided the remains of the feast. The few guests who were still eating fell over themselves and their chairs in their haste to flee as Jack, with arms and legs flailing, rode Humphrey straight at them.

“No! No! Stop, Jack. Stop!” yelled Charlene but her cries were lost amidst the cheering and shouting of the other guests. The great bay horse, although terrified by the racket, saw a stride and brave as a lion, cleared two comatose guests, an upturned chair, the table and the flapping table cloth in a huge soaring leap. Jack Flash, drunk and stoned as he was, had absolutely no chance of staying put. He catapulted over H’s shoulder and nosedived over the table to land in a crumpled heap amongst a pile of discarded food and clothes. Suddenly there was a deathly hush; time seemed to stand still as everyone gazed horror stricken upon Jack's inert body. Charlene was the first to break the spell; she rushed over to Jack and cradled his head gently in her hands.

"Jack! Jack! Darling. Oh my God! Jack! My God! He's dead! DEAD!" she screamed.

Jack Flash opened one eye and winked broadly.

"Get off me, you silly cow!" He rose unsteadily to his feet amidst resounding cheers and limped off with his cronies back to the bar. The whole night seemed to breathe a sigh of relief, the music started up again and the party carried on where it had left off. No one was any the worse for wear except that is, the unlucky bay horse with the crooked white stripe.

Humphrey, frightened by the noise and commotion, landed safely over the table but then kept on galloping. Hundreds of years of domesticity were forgotten as the pumping adrenalin pushed the innate flight mechanism of all prey animals into action. He galloped away from the fearsome noise and bright lights and plunged into the dark night. He galloped blindly in fear, yet even in his panic-stricken state he headed in the general direction of the stables. As he rounded the corner into the stable yard, steel shoes flashing sparks on the tarmac he galloped straight into the bonnet of a large car.

Charlene, discarding her £3,000 Jimmy Choo strappy sandals and running as fast as she could in her tight Valentino dress, followed his trail and eventually found him, distressed and shaking, cowering in the corner of his loose box. She took one look and promptly burst into tears. He was shivering uncontrollably, standing in a pool of blood which was growing bigger by the minute. It was fed by a bright red stream that flowed from a huge gash across his chest and a deep slice in his right forearm above his knee. Charlene, with a quiet calm which she never knew she possessed until that moment, wiped her tears on the back of her hand and ripped the sparkling sash from her beautiful Valentino frock. She tied it tightly around the top of H's front leg above the gaping wound, threw a warm stable rug over his back and rushed into the house to find the telephone. The nearest phone was in the library. Once there, she had complete hysterics as she tried to decipher the number for the vet through her streaming tears.

"I can't find the number," she cried. "Someone help me please." The party was still in full swing outside and the few guests floating through the house were oblivious to what they thought were the histrionics of yet another drunken female. Fortunately, it was a very sober Mrs Beans who, passing the library on her way to bed, heard Charlene's pitiful wailing and came to her rescue.

"Oh my dear, what is the matter? It's not that Jack again, is it, upsetting you? It'll be all the drink too, my dear, and all the other poisons you young people seem to need. I don't know. The youth of today. We never needed all that stuff in my day to enjoy ourselves. I just don't know where it's all going to end. In tears like these and that's for sure."

"Oh Mrs Beans, thank goodness you're here. It's Conker! Jack tried to ride him and he fell off. He's OK but Conker's had an accident. He's bleeding all over the stable floor and I can't find the number for the vet."

"Never you mind, my dear. I'll see to it. You sit down." And Mrs Beans, totally used to dealing with several dramas a day as she battled to keep Jack's chaotic house running smoothly, summoned her organisational skills and vast supply of patience, and took over.

She phoned the vet, found a pair of green wellies by the kitchen door for Charlene, poured them both a stiff whiskey and led the way back to the stables.

Charlene pulled round sufficiently to be able to hold H whilst the vet injected him with painkillers and antibiotics and stitched him up. The vet, Matt, a mid-forties Australian with a kind open face and an unruly thatch of blond hair, joined Mrs Beans in much head shaking and tut tutting about the irresponsibility of some young people with too much money and their blatant disregard for God's creatures. Charlene, feeling horribly guilty, just stroked H's sweating neck, cried silently and felt dreadful.

"This horse is lucky to have escaped with his life." Matt's tanned forehead puckered into a frown. "Another few millimetres deeper and he would have been a goner. As it is he is going to be a long time recovering and he will always bear the scars of this accident.

Charlene's tears doubled in intensity and she choked back a sob.

"Poor poor Conker. It's not his fault he's such a sweet horse. If only Jack hadn't wanted to show off to his friends none of this would have happened." She turned her forget-me-not blue eyes as big as saucers towards

Matt. "He will be all right, won't he? He's had a pretty raw deal here really. He was one of Jack's crazes and now he's lost interest in him and spends all his time sky diving with that horrible Lucy. He's moved on now in typical Jack fashion and doesn't care anymore about Conker — or about me," she added quietly.

Matt thought how stupid Jack Flash must be on two counts as he looked at the beautiful, injured horse and the beautiful, sobbing girl in her torn Valentino dress and the large green wellies.

"Don't worry now. Charlene, isn't it? I'll soon have this horse back to his old self. It was you calling me out so quickly which will make all the difference to his recovery."

"Thank you so much for coming out so quickly and for all your help." Charlene broke the contemplative silence as they leaned over the loose box door. "I'm quite sure you must be ready to go home now but if you would like a cup of coffee, you're more than welcome."

Matt looked down at the beautiful, mascara streaked, tragic face and thought — empty flat or drink with amazing girl? Wise head said, "Busy day tomorrow go home now!" Foolish heart said "No contest!" Matt sighed deeply.

"Stupid heart wins every time!"

"Pardon?"

"Thank you, I would love a drink."

The party was still in full swing but the small utility kitchen was quiet and Matt and Charlene sat on the floor with their backs to the washing machine, deep in conversation, drinking coffee and whiskey chasers, until the streaks of pale dawn filtered surprisingly through the window.

After that night, whenever Matt came on his visits to H, Charlene was always there to lend a helping hand. In fact, the only good thing to come out of that fateful night was that eventually Matt summoned up the courage to invite Charlene out to dinner and they soon became an 'item'. Charlene happily swapped her Jimmy Choos for a pair of pink wellies, adding a splash of glamour and colour to the most gruesome farmyards and bringing a smile to the gloomiest farming countenances as she cheerily accompanied Matt on his rounds.

Over the next few weeks, as H was slowly recovering, Jack never came near. Perhaps it was guilt or perhaps he just didn't care. His records were selling by the millions and he was rapidly rising to superstar status. He went on a long world tour which was a resounding success and amid his brittle busy life he had no time for a scarred old horse.

One drizzling July morning, about a month after that fateful party night, Charlene and Matt drove into the yard on a scheduled veterinary visit to check on Humphrey's progress. They were immediately greeted by a tearful Jenny being comforted by her equally tearful mum.

"Mrs Beans, Jenny, whatever is the matter?" Charlene asked.

"Oh it's dreadful!" choked Mrs Beans. "They've taken that sweet horse away! Mr Flash told Brian to find somewhere for him."

"Don't you worry." Charlene put her arm round the sobbing Jenny. "Jack promised that I could have Conker. He must have forgotten. I'll go and sort it out."

"No! No! You don't understand. Brian called the knackers. They took him early this morning before we were up." Such was the extent of Brian's revenge for the humiliation which he suffered in the fountain all those weeks ago.

"What?" roared Matt "The spite of the man! What a plonker! Where is he? I'll kill him!" He looked with concern at the now three sobbing females! "No worries, girls. I'll ring Mr Edge the knacker man straight away and then I'll find Brian and kill him! Charlene, love. You ring idiot boy Jack and tell him what's happened. I'll ring Mr Edge now, and we'll go pick Conker up and take him to my place."

Charlene and Jenny ran off in the direction of the house. Matt dialled the knacker yard on his mobile.

"Mr Edge? Matt Brown here! We're trying to locate a big bay horse with healing scars on his chest and legs I believe you collected him this morning from Flashlands."

"Well, yes, I did. Brian rang me. He was most insistent that I collected him immediately."

"I'm afraid Brian had no right to do that and it is Mr Flash's express wish that the horse is returned here immediately. It's all been a most dreadful mistake."

There was a deathly hush on the other end of the line. Matt crossed his fingers and hardly dared breathe.

"I'm sorry, Mr Brown, but I'm afraid you're too late. The horse has gone."

“Gone?” breathed Matt. “What d’you mean gone? Has he already been slaughtered?”

Sid Edge narrowed his eyes and looked out of his office window at the bay hunter walking stiffly up the ramp of a large cattle waggon. He glanced down at the wad of fifty pound notes in his hand and took a long pull on his cigarette.

“I’m afraid so. He went with the first batch this morning.”

“Oh I see. Thank you.” Matt slowly pressed the red end call button on his phone and wondered how he was ever going to find the words to tell Charlene.

Chapter Eight

Another long journey, another vehicle. This one a huge rattling monster, speeding Humphrey into yet another chapter of his life. Nearly two years had passed since the hunting accident at the thoughtless hands of Gareth. H still possessed the kind intelligent head with the unusual white crooked blaze and the quality of his ancestors in his breeding but his legs were pretty well shot. They swelled up when he stood overnight in his box and both front tendons were now permanently thickened. In addition, he now had a huge wound running across his chest where he had hit the car bonnet. Despite Matt's valiant attempts at stitching, it was taking a long time to close the deep gouges and the flesh was red and ugly in its healing process. There was another raised scar which ran diagonally across the top of his right foreleg. H was quite thin as he had refused to eat much during his enforced box rest at Flashlands. Although reduced physically to a disfigured shadow of his former self, he bore everything that fate threw at him with all the patience and forbearance which dumb creatures seem to possess during their fragile treaty with the human race. H was still blessed with his generous, trustful nature and although his needs and behaviour may have been misunderstood through sheer ignorance and stupidity, he was never treated with wanton cruelty. That is, until now.

The journey was a long one but at the end of it, as the ramp was dropped, there was a smell of the sea and the eerie cry of wheeling seagulls. H was unloaded and led down a narrow lane through an iron gate and into a small wooden shed. This was one of a line of three and faced three other dilapidated wooden buildings about two metres away across a dusty yard. His stable (if you could call it that) had not been mucked out for weeks and the floor was deep in thick manure and rotting straw. H had to lower his head to avoid banging it on the tin roof. In the corner was a rusting metal bucket of filthy water and a handful of dusty hay to last him the night.

The next morning the shed door was flung open by a thin cadaverous youth with mean eyes and the countenance of a weasel. Over his skinny arm was an old saddle and bridle. He lurched towards the unsuspecting H who immediately received a stinging blow round his head.

"Get back, you great brute!" he shouted and gave the horse a hefty kick in the gut with his oversized Doc Martens.

Unused to such treatment, H shot backwards, half-reared in fear and immediately his head smacked into the tin roof with a resounding crash. The boy laughed.

"Now you stupid git, doesn't that just serve you right!" He rammed a rusty old Pelham bit into H's mouth and slapped the saddle on his back. By this time H was trembling. He hesitated in the doorway for the briefest moment to take in his surroundings as he was being led out and received another kick in the ribs and a jab in the mouth. H didn't know what to do. It seemed as if his every move received some sort of punishment. He rushed through the door and stood uneasily in the dismal dirty yard, quivering with fear.

"We've got a right one 'ere, Spike. Looks a nutter to me." The words came from the tight-lipped mouth of Spike's girlfriend, Callie. A scruffy young girl with close-shaven bright purple hair and a similar mean weasel face. She based her wardrobe and appearance on her hero, Spike, and was often mistaken for his sister. Her obsession with Spike included not only copying his appearance but also his character by extending her naturally mean disposition and cruel streak into added dimensions in order to impress him. "Watch this!" She smacked H round the head and he ran backwards into an old iron bath. They both guffawed loudly. H stood and shook.

"We'll soon teach him who's boss, eh doll! C'mon let's get going." So saying, Spike opened the other shed and led out two thin donkeys. They looked vaguely at H out of big rheumy eyes and stood quietly with heads drooping and long ears splayed. Callie untied a small piebald mare which had been standing quietly tied to a drain pipe, completely disinterested in her surroundings and vaulted onto her back. "OK, I'm ready. Let's go! Are you going to ride that sod?"

"Certainly am!" replied Spike. He vaulted into the saddle, gave H a thwack with a long cutting whip and then screwed him round in tiny circles until he nearly fell over. "That'll show the bugger. C'mon let's go!" He grabbed the two donkeys' reins and hauled them onto either side of him, kicked H in the ribs and set off down the track at a spanking trot, the two donkeys banging their hips into the gate post and the iron gate as they squashed through the narrow opening. At the end of the track they hurtled through a small housing estate, trotted for about a kilometre down a busy main road and then turned onto a beach.

It was mid-morning by this time and the day was unusually sunny and bright. The beach was crowded with holiday makers, mainly families with deck chairs and windbreaks, cricket bats and beach balls. Harassed parents struggled with demanding children, buckets and spades, towels and bags, sand encrusted sandwiches and bottles of drinks. The two donkeys, the bay horse and the piebald pony were kept busy all day trudging up and down 100 metres of sand for 50p a ride. There was no shade and no water. The sand irritated H's unhealed scars and no amount of twitching and tail swishing would get rid of the buzzing clouds of flies. It was late in the afternoon when they finally left the beach and headed wearily through the housing estate and back to the yard. Back in his shed H drank gratefully in great gulps from the dirty water and soon had finished the thin wafer of hay which was thrown at him. He was very tired and still very hungry and the unhealed lacerations on his chest were painfully red and angry.

During that first week, day followed dreadful day. H cowered in his box whenever footsteps approached. He was always greeted by a cuff round the head and a kick in the ribs. His joints became stiffer and stiffer, his legs were permanently swollen, filled with fluid and his wounds became infected and refused to heal properly. He was barely sound as his unshod hooves became split and weakened. In just a week Humphrey's condition worsened considerably and without good food and rest he became thinner and weaker and weaker. The little piebald mare and the two donkeys seemed to be made of sterner stuff for they seemed to manage the daily drudge and being smaller, the meagre rations of hay they received on a night, were just enough to maintain a little body weight.

The children who wanted to ride varied tremendously in their attitudes and behaviour. Many were loud and rough and would kick and kick until H broke into a shambling trot, which was the best he could do and a far cry from the lovely swinging stride which used to cover the miles easily when he was hunting. Now every step seemed a nightmare. He was old and tired and half starved, his eyes were dull and lifeless and his head seemed huge on the end of his scraggy neck.

Some of the other children were, however, shafts of light in that dark week. They cuddled and petted him and brought him carrots and polos until Spike or Callie would frighten them off with a loud shout.

"'Ere you don't be going near that big 'oss on your own. 'E'll bite you!"

Some parents even tut tutted about H's poor state and one vowed to call the RSPCA but he went back to his five-star hotel and forgot.

There was one little boy in particular, Johnny Collins. He appeared on the beach each day with his brown hair in a number 3 crew cut, bright eyes and chirping voice. He always had a titbit which H took carefully from the small palm. Somewhere in the recess of his bemused memory H remembered other tiny people giving him affection and titbits and always speaking cheerily and kindly to him. He snuffled into Johnny's stubbly hair and rested his head on the boy's small shoulder.

"Hey, you know what, mister"? chirped Johnny. "This horse is tired. He needs a rest and he has sore legs and his cuts are bleeding."

"Clear off, kid," growled Spike. "What do you know about it? He's here to do a job of work. There's nothing wrong with him. He's just old and lazy that's all."

"Well I think you're cruel!" retorted Johnny doggedly.

"Look, kid. I said clear off!" Spike approached menacingly. "You've been nothing but a bloody nuisance all day hanging around. Now go on, clear off! Sling yer hook!"

Johnny stood his ground and where older wiser men might have quailed, he shook his tiny fist at Spike's angry bulk.

"You're a horrid bully and not fit to have a nice horse like this. I'm going to tell my dad and he's going to come and knock your block off!" He gave Spike a swift kick on the shin, avoided with all the nimble dexterity of his youth the lunge which Spike made at him, and fled. He paused a suitable distance away from the seething Spike and stuck out his tongue.

"My dad'll come and get you! Just you wait!"

Spike made as if to go after him but thought better of it. He spat a huge globule of spit into the sand and roughly dragged H back into line with the three others.

"What was all that about?" enquired Callie.

"Nowt much! Just some snotty-nosed kid interfering, I've seen him off with a flea in his ear!"

"Little shit!" she observed. "What time we off home? I'm fed up now!"

"We might as well go now. It looks like rain and all the punters are starting to pack up and go."

The rain started in small drips but was soon vertical rods obliterating the view of the grey sea as the forlorn group made their way across the wet sand and onto the road. By the time they arrived back at the yard everything was soaking wet. H, who had a thinner coat than the others, was cold and hungry. Because of his infected wounds, his lack of food and his general poor state, his body heating mechanism was breaking down and his level of immunity was at an all-time low. He was put into his shed, untacked hurriedly, thrown a handful of hay and left to shiver.

"C'mon Spike! Hurry up, I'm freezing." Carrie's voice rose to a plaintive whine.

"This stupid horse doesn't look that good to me! He's shivering!"

"So am I. Shut his shed door, he'll be fine. Now come on let's get back. We can get changed and be down to the pub for early doors."

Spike glanced at the shivering horse standing quietly with his head drooped close to the pile of hay but not eating.

"He's not eating neither!"

"So what! He'll eat later! Now come on or I'm going without you."

The thought of a long wet walk back to the tatty flat they rented in the middle of town was too much for Spike.

"Hold on, you daft bitch! I'm coming!" he slammed the shed door shut and hopped into the van leaving H to his fate.

The next morning, despite an incessant kicking from Carrie's Doc Martens, H was so weak he couldn't rise.

"Spike!" Carrie yelled in frustration." Get yer arse over here. This sod of a horse won't get up!"

Spike now applied his sizeable pair of Doc Martens to H's ribs to try to kick him to his feet. H flinched under every blow and even raised his head and tried desperately to rise. He managed to straighten his forelegs out in front but did not have the strength to push with his hind legs and lever himself up. He crashed back onto the filthy floor where he lay spread-eagled with his head squashed up against the rusting water bucket. Spike gave him another kick out of sheer frustration.

"Bloody thing. We'll have to leave him here today. He's had it anyway. I'll ring the knackers this evening and they can come and collect him. He never was much good. Can't stand the pace! We never should have bought him! What a waste of money! C'mon, let's get these other buggers on the road."

It never occurred to either Spike or Carrie that perhaps if H had been fed properly and cared for he would in fact have lasted a long time and with his kind and generous nature would have given years of useful service.

But then both Spike and Carrie had never been fortunate in their upbringing to know the rewards that love and kindness and generosity can bring. Both had left home at fifteen to escape the continual verbal and physical abuse they suffered in their home lives. Spike from a violent alcoholic father, and Carrie from a lecherous step-father who had turned violent when she had finally found the courage to buy and fit a strong bolt for the inside of her bedroom door to stop his nocturnal wanderings. Carrie found living in the squalid flat with the aggressive Spike a vast improvement on her life in the large detached property overlooking the sea which was formerly her home.

Each night for two long years she had lived in fear of the sound of the squeaking floorboard on the landing and the hoarse whisper, "Carrie darling, it's only Uncle Bill." Huddled, trembling and guilty, she would clutch the beautiful white sheets of Egyptian cotton under her chin until her knuckles were white. But, fine as they were, they offered scant protection from the attentions of her lascivious guardian.

Carrie never understood the final humiliation. That day she finally plucked up enough courage to tell her mother. This well-known model of perfect motherhood rounded on Carrie in uncontrollable fury, called her a little whore and threw her out of the house, and that was that! Carrie's faith in the human race had never been restored and she, with her young and damaged soul, had finally come across the equally damaged Spike. She was devoted to him because he had believed her and nasty as he sometimes could be, at least he didn't live in a life of half-truths and false promises.

Later that morning Johnny made good his threat to Spike and did indeed appear on the beach with his dad. They approached the glowering Spike.

"Hey mister! Where's that big brown horse. What have you done to him? You horrible man!" As he spoke, Johnny gave Spike a pummelling with his small fists.

"Get off, you stupid little brat." Spike pushed him away none too gently and Johnny sprawled in a heap on the damp sand.

"Hey, that's my eight-year-old son you're manhandling. If you need to push anyone find someone your own size." Jim Collins was an ex-international rugby player and he towered over the skinny Spike like a great colossus. "Johnny, you go back to your mum and I'll find out about this horse."

"That kid of yours has been nothing but a bloody nuisance all this week," snapped Spike "Why can't you keep the little bugger under control."

Jim's normally pleasant expression hardened as he took in not only the belligerent Spike and the sulky scruffy girl by his side, but also the two pathetic donkeys and the skinny piebald pony. His friendly blue eyes hardened to flints of stone. Spike watched in morbid fascination the huge fists clenching and unclenching. Jim Collins looked as if he might at any moment smack one of them into his chin. In fact, Spike moved back a couple of paces just in case. However, Jim Collins drew himself up to his full height — a sight which had put fear into many a tough prop forward in the past — and said quietly. "I've met your type before. You're not fit to own an animal and it strikes me that, for reasons which escape me, you get pleasure from bullying the helpless. Now how about bullying me?" There was silence for a long moment. Spike shuffled uncomfortably from foot to foot. There was no way he wanted any sort of argument with this huge menacing stranger. After all he might hurt himself.

"Just as I thought. You're like all bullies, in reality you're just a coward." So saying, he cast Spike a pitying glance, turned on his heel and strode away.

Spike breathed a huge sigh of relief and then laughed loudly, his confidence returning as he saw the huge man collect his wife and child and prepare to leave the beach.

"Well what a wimp! I saw him off all right, eh Carrie, luv."

"Mmm." Carrie knew better than to disagree with Spike so she gave him a sly grin. "You certainly did! You're great you are! You're dead tough you are! He won't be back in a hurry."

"No, I stood up to him proper, I did. He didn't want to tangle with the likes of me. He knows I could 'ave give 'im what for if I'd felt like it. Come on, you lazy cow, let's get back to work."

Near the end of the day, when the sun was a great red orb resting on the sea, they made their way back to the stables. However, as they turned into the yard they received a nasty shock. Standing in a forbidding row to greet them were three uniformed men. Two were policemen and one was an RSPCA officer. Jim Collins was by their side. In the shed Spike could just make out someone bending over the prostrate bay horse. In the face of all this officialdom Spike resorted, as he always had in the past, to blustering and lies.

"'Ere what d'you think you're doing on my property and who's that interfering with my horse? You can't come on 'ere without a warrant."

"The horse, sir, if you can call the poor pathetic creature that, is going where you will never be able to hurt it again," replied one of the policemen. "Our main concern, however, is how you came in possession of a number of items, believed stolen, which we have found in your home which was searched this afternoon. For which I can assure you we had a warrant." The young policeman couldn't help the suggestion of a satisfying smile flickering briefly across his face. "We've been watching you for some time, sir, and want you to accompany us down to the station for further questioning. You will also be charged with cruelty and neglect under The Protection of Animals Act." He then read, to the open-mouthed Spike, his rights.

Spike was duly led away with Carrie trailing miserably in his wake.

Jim Collins stared stonily at them as they passed.

"You interfering old git." shouted Spike "I'll 'ave you yet."

"I think not, young man!" Jim Collins seemed totally unperturbed. "If you're going to throw your weight around I suggest you don't do it in front of a Detective Chief Inspector! What a piece of luck that I chose this splendid resort for a few days break."

For once in his life Spike was at a total loss for words. His skinny shoulders slumped and he allowed himself, without a murmur, to be bundled into the squad car, which was waiting in the lane. Callie watched the car disappear down the track and then stomped to the van and followed in its wake.

"Now, Mr Collins, I'll go and organise a horsebox to remove these poor creatures." It was the RSPCA inspector who spoke. "I've been in touch with the lady from the local rest home for retired horses. These two donkeys and the pony look as if they've earned honourable retirement and she has a place for them.

At that moment the vet appeared at the shed door.

"I'm afraid this poor old lad has had it. He's so ill and weak I don't think he'll ever get up again. I'll go and get the drugs from the car. I think it would be kinder to put him out of his misery. What a cruel waste of a life. My job is about healing animals not killing them." He walked with heavy tread towards the gate and on reaching it was met by a small whirlwind which hurtled round the corner and straight into him.

"Steady on there, young man. What's the hurry?"

"Oh, I'm so sorry." Johnny's mother was in hot pursuit. "I just couldn't keep him any longer. He's so desperate to find out about the horse. Is everything going to be all right?"

"I'm afraid the prognosis is not so good," said the vet kindly and continued on towards his car. Johnny caught site of the prostrate bay body and dived into the shed.

"Jim, what's happening?"

"Well that cruel little bully and thief will hopefully learn his lesson if justice is dispensed as it should be."

"What about these poor animals?" she asked. "Oh, the poor things! How could anyone be so cruel. Look how thin they are! I had no idea they were so bad. I thought Johnny was exaggerating as usual! I've brought them some carrots." Jane Collins proceeded to feed carrots to the donkeys and the pony. They raised their tired heads and the donkeys pricked up their huge ears as they savoured such an unexpected treat.

"Well, my love," said Jim, "I know these three, look pretty bad, but that's nothing compared to the other poor thing in there." Jane looked searchingly at her husband and then walked over to the shed. Her heart lurched at the scene before her. Johnny was sitting in the filthy rotting straw with the stilled bay head cradled in his arms. Tears were rolling down his pale cheeks and dropping onto the horse's forehead, making tiny wet furrows in the matted hair.

"Please don't die, horse. Oh, please don't die," he muttered over and over again. "I don't want you to die. I don't want you to die. I know you can get better if you try. Only please don't die."

Jane looked up at the silent vet with the lethal drugs and syringe in his hand.

"Oh Lord!" she choked. "Is there nothing we can do?"

Chapter Nine

The vet looked at the small boy and his concerned parents.

"This is the hardest part of my job but I hold out no hope for this horse and still feel it would be kinder to put him out of his misery."

Jane Collins looked at her distraught son and the dying horse and decided she would not think of giving up without a fight.

"What if we try to do something right now and just give him another night." She looked pleadingly at her husband. "Oh come on, Jim, for goodness sake! Look at them both. What have we got to lose?"

Jim looked and his mind flew unbidden to other times on the rugby field when he was young and things looked hopeless and giving up was never in his vocabulary.

"Absolutely nothing to lose! You're quite right love. Let's give the horse another night. What do you say, Mr, er, sorry, I don't even know your name."

"Myers, Giles Myers. Pleased to meet you." He held out his hand.

Jim shook the proffered hand. "What a shame we had to meet in such harrowing circumstances. Is there anything at all that you can do?"

"Well I don't hold out any hope but if you're adamant and as the young lad is so very upset, I suppose

I could give the horse isotonic fluid to help rehydrate him. It might just see him through the night. He also needs high quality alfalfa which he needs to eat in a small handful, every few hours. If you can persuade him that is. He certainly can't eat any more of that foul dusty hay. He needs protein now. He's in such a bad state his starved body has been breaking down the protein from his muscles and vital organs. He will be lucky to avoid any internal damage even if he survives. I'm sorry to be such a portent of doom but I don't want to raise any false hopes. You must understand that if there's no change by the morning I can't, in all fairness to the animal, put off the inevitable any longer."

Giles duly gave H the fluid, holding the bag high and shaking his head sadly when the horse never even moved at the insertion of the catheter into his jugular vein. He reiterated that he thought the horse was too weak to survive, that his will to live seemed to have deserted him and that he doubted very much that he would even last the night. He rang the rest home for horses and asked if they could spare a bag of alfalfa and a bale of straw until they could get a delivery from the local feed merchant.

After he had left with the reassurance that he would return at eight the next morning, Jim tried to persuade Johnny it was time to go home.

"C'mon son, we've done all we can now. We can come back first thing in the morning."

Johnny was having none of it. Nothing would persuade him to desert his equine friend and when his father tried to gently prise him away Johnny became quite hysterical.

In the end Jane went back to the hotel and came back with coffee, soup and sandwiches, car rugs and pillows and blankets to make her two boys comfortable for the night. She found an old waterproof jacket and a dog rug in the car which she tenderly placed over H's prone body.

Later in the evening a lady introducing herself as Felicity, from the rest home for horses, came round with some old stable rugs, six bags of Alpha A and three bales of straw in the back of an old pickup. She was a huge woman who advanced into the dismal yard like a great galleon in full sail running before the wind. She arrived at just the right time, when spirits were at their lowest ebb and all the positive hope of a few hours earlier seemed to have evaporated into the chilly night. In silence and with a feline grace which belied her size, she knelt close to the horse and the small boy and cradling the big bay head, blew slowly down H's nostrils and whispered strange sounds in his ears. She produced an exotic-smelling ointment which she soothed on all his festering wounds and she moved her fingers in circular patterns across his body. The air seemed to crackle with energy as his muscles twitched under her electric touch. At one point H raised his head and looked directly at her. She held his gaze and then whispered something unintelligible and his head thudded back onto the straw. The Collins family were mesmerised. Johnny finally broke the spell.

"Misses, are you one of those horse whispers — like in the film."

Felicity laughed, a deep infectious chuckle. "Ah yes, *The Horse Whisperer* — Robert Redford — I wish."

She gathered her voluminous skirts around her, rose smoothly to her feet and with a dazzling, all-encompassing smile, swept out of the door.

They stared after her in disbelief.

"What an unusual woman!" said Jane.

"Very weird," admitted Jim.

"A proper horse whisperer! How awesome is that!" exclaimed Johnny and promptly fell asleep. One small hand was still spread on H's forehead and the other clutched a piece of black mane.

Neither horse nor boy stirred until a shaft of light crept through the rotten planking of the shed catching a host of dust particles in a golden swirl.

By some miracle H was still alive. Perhaps it was the strange administrations of the whispering Felicity. Perhaps it was the comfort and kind words of a small boy or perhaps in the great machinations of the universe, it was not yet his time. Whatever the reason Giles could not quite believe his eyes when he arrived as promised at eight the next morning to be greeted by a tired yet triumphant Collins family trio. Not only was the horse against all odds still alive but he even managed to raise his head to drink some water from the bucket Jim held and even slowly chewed a few mouthfuls of the alfalfa which Felicity had brought the previous night.

"Well I'll be… I was sure this horse was a goner. I've never seen a horse as bad as that recover before. Life never ceases to surprise me! Well done, you lot! I would have given him up for lost. Mind you," Giles' kindly face puckered into a frown, "we're still not out of the woods yet. Not by a long way. We have to get this horse onto his feet if he is to survive."

With much pushing and pulling and by banking wedges of straw around him, they managed to get H to a more upright position and he made a supreme effort and staggered to his feet only to sink back down again as his weak legs gave way. After that all energy seemed to desert him and he once more lay flat out, unmoving on the straw-scattered floor.

Giles shook his head. "It's no good folks. I think we're going to lose him."

"NO! NO!" Johnny refused to give up. "C'mon, you silly horse. GET UP!" He tugged at H's mane but the only response was a twitch of an ear and a feeble movement of his head. "Dad! Dad, you've got to help him," he cried.

Jim Collins was deep in thought. "What about some sort of a sling?" He directed his question to Giles. "I'm sure I've seen films with big animals supported by slings to keep them upright. Would it work for him?"

"It might do. Sometimes we can do it for horses with leg fractures in order to immobilise them and to relieve the strain. This could be a much shorter process, for only a few hours, until we could get some food into him and he can stand on his own. Is it worth it, that's the thing? This is not an expensive race horse or competition horse worth tens of thousands of pounds. In fact there is no guarantee that he will ever be fit for anything much ever again, even if he recovers. My professional advice is to put him out of his misery now."

"No way!" Jane and Johnny chorused in unison.

"C' mon, were not giving up now!" Jane was adamant. "You guys get a sling sorted and we'll stay on a few more days to look after him."

"Dad, I know he'll get better. If we get him on his feet I know I can get him to eat and then he can go to Uncle Stephen. He's got loads of grass." With all the optimism of youth, Johnny had the whole thing sorted. "C'mon Dad, where's the problem."

"Uncle Stephen trains racehorses and I'm sure he won't want a crock on his hands."

At this moment of indecision, the stately galleon that was Felicity appeared at the shed door.

"Now how is my patient this morning? Survived the night I see. C'mon you lot, stop gawping and let's get him on his feet. Giles, go and get a block and tackle and your veterinary sling. Mr Collins I've brought hooks and my drill so get drilling and set these hooks up on this beam here. Chop, chop! This horse is going to survive and it's down to us. So get moving!"

Johnny ran to her and flung his arms around the huge waist. "Thank you! Thank you! I knew you'd come back just when we needed you. You're awesome, you are!"

"Mm, I've been called many things in my life but awesome is not one of them! But thank you, young man, you're not so bad yourself." She patted Johnny's bristly head. "C'mon everyone, let's get going!

With the best will in the world it still took two hours to fetch all the gear they needed. To slide the broad webbing sling under H's prone body was a mammoth task and only achieved with much huffing and puffing and brute strength on the part of Felicity, Jim and Giles.

The pulley ropes were fitted through the hooks on the beam and attached to the sling.

"Right now, everyone, this is the tricky bit. We must try and support the horse and guide him to his feet as the ropes begin to take the strain and make sure he doesn't panic." Felicity with her crackling energy was in charge. "Giles, you and Jim start to haul on the pulley ropes. Let's hope the weight doesn't bring this rickety shambles down around our ears. Jane, you and I will push from the far side to keep the horse straight and young Johnny, you stay by his head. Be careful of those front hooves though in case he starts thrashing about. All set? Now just wait one second will you."

Felicity moved her fingers once more over H's prostrate head and blew in his nostrils. He immediately lifted his head and started to struggle to rise. "OK everyone, this is it! Now!"

The ropes creaked and groaned as everyone pulled or pushed with all their might and H's hooves scrabbled around as they tried to gain a purchase on the shed floor. Somehow the horse seemed to know, as the people surely did, that this was his last chance to survive. He did not give up his struggling and neither did they, until at last he was upright with his hooves resting on the floor but the majority of his weight taken up by the ropes and the sling.

"We did it! We did it!" Johnny was ecstatic. He took H's head in his hands and smothered him with kisses.

"Right now, young man," It was Giles' turn to take charge. "This dreadful shed — I refuse to call it a stable, needs a thorough clean out and the new straw putting down. The patient needs alfalfa. One pound every four hours for the next two days. After that, if he's eating up, we can slowly increase the amounts and decrease the number of feeds so that in about a week's time he's getting four pounds every eight hours. Hopefully then depending how he is, he can go onto ad lib and have a little fresh cut grass every day. He needs fresh water available at all times. We can set up a bucket holder here and attach it to the shed side. He needs little and often or you'll give him colic. I'll set up more electrolytes. I can hook the bags to the beam. Let's hope it doesn't collapse the whole shed! The rest is up to him, if he wants to survive, he will start to eat. I'll call in again tomorrow morning and when he's a bit more stable I'll give him some antibiotics to help those wounds heal. Call me on my mobile if you need me."

Giles paused in the doorway and looked back at the tableau of the Collins family and the indomitable Felicity. Weary anxious faces surrounding the drooping bay head. His serious face cracked into a broad grin. "My God! What a team!"

Jim accompanied him to his car.

"What about the cost of all this? I know veterinary services don't come cheap."

"I'm sure we can all come to some arrangement," replied Giles. "I can try sending the bill to that young thug, probably care of Her Majesty's pleasure but I don't hold out much hope that he can possibly pay it. If I get paid just for the medications that will do me. My time you can have for free. Man cannot live by money alone. I've been a vet now for over twenty years and it's done my cynical old heart good to see a young whippersnapper like your son give up his holiday for a sick old horse. The world can't be that bad Mr Collins as long as there are caring people about like you and your family and Felicity. What's that famous saying? Something like 'The only way evil can succeed is when good men do nothing'? Well there are lots of good men out there and women and children who won't let evil win, not in the great scheme of things, not overall. Oh well - philosophy lecture over! I've a lot of visits to make, so see you tomorrow." With a self-effacing shrug of his shoulders and a wry smile he was gone.

Jim watched his car disappear up the lane then slowly turned back towards the dismal shed with the fight for life within it. He suddenly felt a surge of hope for the horse and a great pride in his young son.

All that day and the next Johnny hardly left H's side. He hand-fed him the alfalfa religiously every four hours, and held buckets of water for him to drink. The team lowered the horse from the sling every four hours and allowed him to rest on the straw for a few hours before struggling to get him upright again. Slowly, over the two days H began to eat more and to take a slight interest in his surroundings and finally towards the end of the second day he struggled to his feet and stood unsteadily for a few moments before sinking wearily again into the deep straw bed. The third night Jane insisted that Johnny went back to the hotel for a good night's sleep and Felicity said she would stay with the horse. Early the following morning, H whinnied softly as they arrived, his eyes were a little brighter and he pricked his ears as he ate. He was a little stronger and was able to stand for longer without the sling. The following day the sling was discarded altogether and H was able to take all his own weight and move, albeit slowly, around the shed.

Giles made frequent visits and by the end of the second week declared that H was strong enough to be moved but would not recover fully — if indeed he ever could — until he was able to graze on some good pasture next spring.

"That's when good old Dr Green should work its magic," he proclaimed to the team as they stood before him in the yard. Johnny was holding the end of H's lead rope and had just walked him a few metres up and down the lane as part of his recovery programme. The bay horse was still painfully thin, his head still looking far too big for his scraggy hollow neck to support.

"Well!" said Giles counting the ribs on H's still thin and wasted frame. "You've all done a marvellous job. I still can't quite believe that a horse in his condition has survived the fight. He still has a long way to go but he's definitely on the mend. He needs somewhere now where he can be turned out every day to get his old joints moving again. What about this uncle of yours Johnny, this race horse trainer? Can he go there?"

"C'mon Dad, I'm sure Uncle Stephen will help."

Jim wasn't too sure. "My brother is a very busy man with all those racehorses to train. I don't think he'll have the time or inclination to take on an invalid." Jim forgot to mention that although they only lived a few miles apart they'd not spoken to each other for ages, not exactly fallen out but just grown apart over the years. He hated the thought of asking his arrogant successful elder brother for a favour but looking down at Johnny's expectant face, he capitulated. "Well, I suppose after all this effort we've been through, it might be worth a try."

"I only wish I could take him at the rest home," exclaimed Felicity more aware than any of them of the internal struggle going on in Jim's mind. "But I am absolutely choc-a-block. The little pony and the two donkeys are doing just fine but I am bursting at the seams." She looked down at her huge frame and smiled ruefully. "Mm, in more ways than one I know."

"Who exactly owns this horse now?" Jane asked reasonably. "I'm not sure how we stand legally if we just take him off somewhere."

"Ah, I can help you there." It was Giles who answered. "I spoke to the RSPCA this morning. They were enquiring about how he was doing. The horse is now under their ownership and protection. They will be very happy to take my advice on the best way forward for him and it just so happens that I have a transfer of ownership document with me for you to sign, Jim, and for me to endorse."

"Great!" Jim smiled ruefully as he looked at the pathetic creature in front of him which was about to become his responsibility.

"Oh, for God's sake, Jim." Jane was losing patience. "Just get the bloody thing signed and then get on your mobile and ring Stephen. I'll do it if you like." With that, she dived into her bag, retrieved a pen and signed the document with a flourish. There, that's done! Now give me your mobile."

"Well done, Mum. Now, Dad, it's your turn! Please ring Uncle Stephen."

Jim had to laugh. "What can a man do in the face of such bullies?" He looked fondly at his wife and son. "OK! OK! I give in, but I'll ring Stephen this evening when he won't be so busy and will hopefully be in a receptive mood."

"Thanks, Dad," chirped Johnny after they had waved goodbye to Giles and Felicity and were standing once more with H in the small shed. "I love this horse, Dad. He's such a fighter and Uncle Stephen will love him too."

"Mm." Jim was non-committal as he watched H munch methodically through his pile of fresh grass.

The next morning saw a new visitor leaning over the stable door, impatiently scrutinising the scrawny bay. This was Uncle Stephen, who had called in on his way from Lambourn to an important race meeting in Newcastle, under duress, and only after much persuasion from his brother and more than a few tears from Johnny.

The pitiful sight before him compounded his worst fears.

"My dear little brother!" His accent was crisp and cool. "This is not a horse! This is a poor collection of antique bones! I doubt this poor wretched thing will ever recover!"

"But Uncle Stephen. He's so much better now. You should have seen him two weeks ago. Giles says he'll get better, and I sat up with him for two nights and everyone thought he was going to die except me and Felicity and he's so sweet and he's fought so hard to get better and I'll come and muck him out and muck out all the other horses as well and he just needs another chance and I'll love you for ever if you take him…"

Johnny's torrent of words dried up as he finally ran out of breath, and under Stephen's cool grey gaze he shuffled uncomfortably and hung his head. He looked so totally forlorn that Stephen found himself saying, "Don't look so despairing, old chap, let's have a closer look at him, shall we?" Stephen entered the shabby shed and ran his hands down H's forelegs. Immediately he had the strongest feeling of déjà vue as if he had done exactly the same thing to this same horse in a different place a long time ago. He carefully examined both swollen front legs, especially the bowed tendon on the near fore and gazed thoughtfully at the crooked white stripe on the horse's head.

"Good Lord! This just can't be! Surely not! But then he is the right height and age and there's no mistaking those forelegs and his markings. Well, I'll be damned. I'm sure I've seen this horse before. In fact, I wanted to buy him at Drumalee sales last year in Ireland. It's a long story." Stephen Collins' eyes narrowed in grey anger as he tenderly patted the scrawny neck. "How was he ever reduced to this terrible state? My God, I'd like to get my hands on the people who did this to him."

"Oh, Uncle Stephen, isn't that amazing!" Johnny jumped up and down in excitement. "I found him working on the beach and he was in an awful state." Johnny and his father proceeded to explain between them the horse's short history as they knew it and Stephen told them how he had made the trip to the scrap yard of the two Irish men and how he had just missed bidding for him at the sales.

"Well, Johnny my lad, let's take the old boy home and see what we can do for him. I liked him then and I like him now, despite his sorry state and you're right, he certainly is a fighter! The least we can do is restore him to some sort of fitness again and if he never works again then he can be turned out with the young stock. He might even instil a bit of sense into them."

Johnny leapt at his uncle and gave him a big bear hug.

"Thank you! Thank you! Uncle Stephen. You are a real star! Can I come and see him lots?"

Stephen's stern expression cracked and the grey ice melted for just a fraction as he felt the unaccustomed warmth from his young nephew. Recently and painfully divorced from a childless marriage, the thought crossed his mind that young Johnny and his family around his home might not be as awful as he had feared.

"I'll send a lad for him in the morning."

"Can I go with him?" asked Johnny

"I see no reason why not as long as Jim and Jane agree."

"No problem. We're going home tomorrow anyway and I'll come down and pick him up later on," said Jim." But don't forget, son, its back to school on Monday." Johnny pulled a face and then had a thought.

"What's his name? We have to call him something. They just seemed to call him the brute or the sod! We can't call him that."

"Most certainly not. I think his name was Red something. I'll see if I can find the old catalogue from the sales." Stephen patted Johnny's head.

"You know what?" said Jane thoughtfully after they had said friendly goodbyes to Stephen and watched his sleek car glide smoothly down the road, "I have a strong feeling that this horse is going to have a big effect on our lives in more ways than one."

The next morning found H being loaded into yet another horsebox. Johnny led him slowly and carefully up the ramp. His hooves didn't make a sound on the rubber matting and he tucked into a huge net of sweet smelling hay as he travelled.

Johnny was awestruck.

"Awesome!" he exclaimed. This was his favourite word at the moment. "This is the smartest, most awesome horsebox ever!" It was indeed a giant of a vehicle and H looked very small and slightly pathetic standing in one of the six partitions.

Stephen Collins' head lad, Terry, was supervising the journey down to Lambourn. He was very tiny with a shock of red hair which stuck out in all conceivable directions. He patted H kindly and spoke cheerily to him in his soft Irish brogue.

"Come on, old son, let's be having you. For sure, someone should be shot for what they've done to you. 'Tis a rough old time you've had. But it will all change now, my lad, so it will."

Johnny sat next to him in the cab, chattering constantly throughout the journey.

"Why are you so small and what's your name?"

The young man laughed. “Well, young whippersnapper! I’m small because I’m a jockey and I have to be small and light so the horse will run faster.”

“Wow! I want to be a jockey when I grow up.”

“Mm. Sure, it’s not as glamorous as some people might think but I love it, so I do!”

“What’s your name?”

“Well now that would be Terrence, but Tops they call me, for short. Carrot tops for long. Tis all because of this.” He pointed ruefully at his unruly hair.

“Wow! I want hair like that when I grow up!”

“No, my boy. Somehow, I don’t think that you will!”

They chatted companionably. Johnny in complete awe sitting high up in the cab with the cheerful Tops beside him who answered his never-ceasing questions about racing and horses with infinite patience. Johnny then told Tops all about finding H on the beach and the ensuing fight for his life.

“You know what I be thinking?” said Tops as they turned into the stable yard at Redwoods. “I’m thinking that I have a strong feeling that this horse here that we’ve just brought home is going to have a big effect on our lives in more ways than one, so he is.”

Johnny looked up in amazement. “Mum said exactly the same. Awesome!”

Chapter Ten

H was now known as Conker, after Stephen had managed to trace his name as Red Conker from the old sale catalogue. His new home was a far cry from the scruffy yard he had just left. His tiny dilapidated shed was now transformed into a big airy loose box with thick rubber matting and clean crisp shavings. His loose box was half way down one side of a large square of boxes which faced a bright green lawn in the centre of which was a life-size statue of a bronze horse. The great stallion Rajah's Moon, who Stephen Collins had trained to win over twenty races and who now stood at The National Stud and was worth a king's ransom in stud fees. Between the lawn and the boxes was a wide gravel pathway. Both lawn and pathway were as clean as a whistle without a blade of hay or wisp of a shaving in sight. Everywhere was clean and tidy, the paintwork was shining and two stone archways faced each other across opposite sides of the square. One led out onto the driveway and the other led to Stephen's imposing lonely house and the jockeys' quarters. The yard and driveway were surrounded by acres of paddocks all bordered by sparkling white post and rails fencing. The two, one hundred-year-old giant Redwood Trees which gave the place its name, planted by the Edwardians, stood proud sentinels alongside the square stone pillars of the gateway. The whole place had an air of prosperity and efficiency which indeed reflected accurately enough Stephen's character and considerable talent as a trainer.

After a month of good grass and gentle exercise on the horse-walker three times a week, H began to look more like a proper horse. He appeared perfectly sound to Tops and Stephen when he was trotted up in hand by young Johnny on one of his frequent visits.

"Well!" exclaimed Stephen "This old horse looks as if he might do a job after all. Why don't you have a sit on him tomorrow, Tops, after the second lot come back and let's see how he behaves. If he's OK I think it might be a good idea if we taught my young nephew to ride. What do you think?"

"Wow!" shrieked Johnny. "Awesome!" Johnny had spent as much time as he could at Uncle Stephen's. He spent most of his half term holidays on the yard and true to his word had mucked out H's box and many others religiously. He hero-worshipped Tops and had struck up a great friendship with Uncle Stephen who, against all odds, had become quite accustomed to his never-ending questions and cheerful company. He even found that when his little brother and his charming wife came to pick up their son he had more in common with them than he would have dreamed possible. He came to look forward to their company and his beautiful house seemed not so lonely when they were around.

Seven-thirty the next morning saw an exuberant H and a grinning Tops bouncing through the archway and up the drive to the gallops. H was thrilled to be out again, wondering if hounds would be around the next corner as he pranced and snorted and shied at imaginary monsters in the verges.

"Hey, now then, but you're a silly old horse y'are," laughed Tops "Sure 'tis very full of yourself this morning y'are. Steady on there. Whoa, Conker my lad, whoa there." H snorted into the fresh breeze and bucked as he felt the springy grass beneath him. Tops shortened his reins and chuckled, his brown face wrinkling into a wide grin. "Now then, don't you think you can be dumping poor Terrence into the dust." He immediately began to sing at the top of his voice. "Bam! Bam! Bam! Bam! Another one bites the dust! And another one! And another one! Another one bites the dust." H flicked his ears and put in another buck. "Now then, old fella, 'tis obvious that y' have no appreciation of Mr Mercury and his amazing music. Let's give you a bit of a stretch to get the wind out of your sails. But 'tis no good t' be galloping your legs off. For sure, you haven't been ridden for a long time and 'tis not as fit as you think y'are!" Indeed, by the time H had slowly trotted a furlong he was huffing and puffing. Tops drew him to a halt and walked quietly back down the gallops towards home. As they walked under the archway into the yard they were met by an enquiring Stephen.

"Now then, Terrence." He was the only person to call Tops by his proper name. "How has Conker behaved?"

"To be sure, he's a delight, as good as gold. He has a mouth like silk, so he has, and someone along the line has taken the time and trouble to school him well."

"Ah. What about the bucking?" queried Stephen.

"Oh that! T'was nothing." Tops realised that Mr Collins, never missing a thing, must have been watching their progress through his binoculars. "Just a little bit of high spirits, feeling the grass under his feet, so he is. I doubt that he's been ridden properly for many a month. All things considered, he has the manners of a saint."

"Mmm," mused Stephen. "That's very interesting. I must say I had my doubts considering where he came from. Still, we'll see how he goes. Perhaps I've got myself a bargain after all."

The next morning, light had only just streaked the navy sky with thin bands of rose when H, having been fed by Tops earlier, was tacked up and led out of his stable. "Right lads, let's get a move on!" Stephen called as he appeared through the archway. He strode up to H and swung himself easily into the saddle. Not for Stephen watching all his horses from the comfort of his Range Rover like a lot of other trainers. He always rode out with one lot each day, loving the smell and the sound, reawakening memories of the days when he too was a raw young jockey riding a powerhouse of muscle into the dawn.

All around the yard lads were hastily vaulting onto their wafer-thin racing saddles as the fit horses plunged and fidgeted in the frosty air. Their warm breath coiled into thin grey wraiths as they blew and snorted and stamped with impatience. H stood like a rock whilst Stephen watched each of the twelve horses circling once around the gravel before leaving the yard for the gallops. His eagle eyes missed nothing. One lad was made to shorten his stirrups even further, one was made to change the horse's bit and another horse was sent back into its box because it was slightly lame. Eventually all the horses were bouncing down the drive with H and Stephen bringing up the rear.

Humphrey didn't mind when he was taken a different route to the others, a short cut which found him positioned near the top of the first all-weather gallop. Stephen watched carefully as groups of two and three horses pounded up the hill past him. H fidgeted a little at first after all he was used to hunting and galloping along with the others. However, Stephen was a sympathetic horseman and he spoke quietly. "Now old son, steady there. You'll have to learn to be patient at this job. I have work to do," he reassured his mount with frequent pats until H understood that he was meant to stand quietly and not follow the herd.

Each morning followed a similar pattern. H and Stephen watched the horses circle the yard and then followed in their wake down the drive until turning away to take the short cut to the gallops. Some days they went with the Dawn Patrol, as the lads called it, and other days with the second or third string later in the morning. Occasionally Stephen's place in the saddle was taken by Tops. The days slid by into weeks and with the best of treatment and good food H began to look and feel like his old self again.

One chilly morning when Christmas had come and gone and the square of grass was covered in a thick blanket of white virgin snow transforming Rajah's Moon overnight from bronze to grey, a new horse arrived. Tops alighted from the cab of Stephen's pale blue and silver horsebox. It rocked and swayed alarmingly beneath crashing hooves, and a cacophony of sound of snorting and squealing emanated from within. Enquiring heads and pricked ears appeared over the top of each stable door in the yard.

"'Tis a bloody demon thing that y'are," muttered Tops uncharacteristically as he ran round to undo the ramp. "That was some dreadful trip, so it was! Come on lads, give us a hand with this beast here before it wrecks the whole of the box, so it will." The ramp was quickly lowered and Tops squeezed round the partition and untied the halter rope.

"Right lads, when I say 'Now', undo the partition as quick as y'like and stand back. OK, ready and — NOW!" A huge chestnut cannonball launched itself from the top of the ramp and in a whirlwind of copper and flying hooves he lashed out, sending a shower of snow and gravel flying in all directions. With rolling white eyes and covered in sweat flecked with white foam, he whirled round and round, nearly dragging the unfortunate Tops off his feet. "Be Jesus!" panted Tops. "Come on, lads. I need some anchorage here, so I do. Let's get him into a box before he should be killing someone." With much swearing and cursing and dodging teeth and hooves every stride, it took three of them to eventually get the horse into a large loose box. Once in there he proceeded to box walk, round and round in determined agitation making a deep circular track in the shavings like a great big mechanical roundabout horse on a non-stop merry-go-round.

"Mother of God!" said Tops. "To be sure, we've a right one here. I wonder what the divil's happened to him to make him be so afraid. Let's feed him some haylage and leave him be, to settle."

The new arrival was called Nutcracker, a name which Tops thought very appropriate as he explained to Stephen as they leaned over the loose box door the following morning

"You know, boss, 'tis a feeling I have that just plain old Crackers would suit him the better. Sure, I thought he was going to kill us when we unloaded him yesterday."

"I have to say Terrence, he is a bit on the wild side." Tops nearly exploded at the 'a bit' but decided to stay cool and sing a few bars of Lou Reed's *Take a Walk on the Wild Side*, instead.

"Great song that. The tenor sax in the middle is amazing." Tops thought again that the boss never ceased to surprise him. "However, this horse is really swift and a fantastic jumper. He's won three National Hunt races already — but and it's a big but — that was over a year ago and then he decided to throw in the towel. He won't even approach the track now. As soon as he gets to a race meeting he goes ballistic from the moment he gets off the lorry. This is his last chance, I'm afraid. He's here because I rather took pity on him at the sales last week. It's a gamble, I know, but he has already put two jockeys in hospital and his next journey was going to be to the knackers. He's such a magnificent animal, it seemed such a waste."

Nutcracker, as if to defy these kind sentiments by pressing his own self-destruct button, rushed at the two men his head snaking over the door, ears flat back and teeth snapping. Both men, however, stood their ground and Tops growled a warning.

"Grrr! Get on with you! You're an evil beast so y'are. It'll take more than a few nasty faces to frighten the likes of us so it will."

Nutcracker, expecting a fearful retreat or at the very least a crack around the head, pulled up short in surprise. His ears flicked briefly forward as he listened to the soft growl and for a brief moment the wild eyes cleared, he arched his neck and blew in Top's outstretched palm. However, as if terrified of this brief olive branch of peace, he then whirled round, flattened his ears again and lashed out furiously, his shoes striking the stable door just below the men's faces with a resounding thud. This time both men jumped backwards.

"Well," contemplated Stephen ruefully. "No one said this was going to be easy. I seem to have got a real screwball here. Let's give him a few weeks and see how we get on. I'll leave you in charge of him, Terrence, with your experience and calming influence but be very careful. I can't have anybody injured. This job is difficult enough and a high risk sport as you very well know." Tops smiled ruefully and subconsciously touched his right thigh, the femur held together by a steel pin. He remembered his dreadful fall at Becher's in The National ten years ago which had brought a premature end to his blossoming racing career.

"Even with the sweetest horses," Stephen continued, "accidents can happen and people get injured even in the normal run of things. No point tempting fate too much.

No horse is worth that much, and at the moment, I would say this horse is quite capable of killing someone."

"Don't you be worrying y'self, boss. I'll take great care, so I will and maybe we'll try a little kindness and patience and see how we get on."

"I wonder," mused Stephen as he turned away, "just what has happened to this horse to make him hate the human race so much? By the way, why not put him in a box next to something he can't upset. Put him next to Conker. Maybe he'll be able to teach him some manners. I certainly don't want him next to my best runners. Can't have them upset."

So it was, that Humphrey had the noisy nasty chestnut as a nuisance neighbour.

The first few days were a constant battle. Poor old Tops found himself on the unforgiving ground more times than he was in the saddle. It took two men leading and one following, cracking a lunge whip, to persuade Nutcracker even to leave the yard. After the second week, as long as he was in the middle of the string, he managed to trot down the drive, past the giant redwoods and as far as the gallops. However, no amount of persuasion, neither stick nor carrot, would get him to set foot on the all-weather surface. As soon as his hooves touched the surface he would rear and whip round like a spinning top. Then one day the inevitable happened. He reared so high in his fury and frustration that he flipped over backwards, pinning the long-suffering Tops beneath him. Stephen, swivelling his binoculars from his last group of galloping horses towards the fracas, swore under his breath and kicked Humphrey into a gallop down the hill. They arrived as Tops was slowly getting to his feet, bruised and battered but amazingly unhurt.

"My God, lad. Are you all right?"

"I am that, Mr Collins, sir" he smiled ruefully. "I feel as if I've been run over by twenty trucks, but sure I'll survive, so I will. 'Tis a good job I had my crash hat on for I'm sure that the brute stood on my head on purpose, so he did, as he got up!"

Tops did indeed have a nasty gash on the side of his face from which the blood was flowing freely.

"I think that might need a stitch or two. I'll get one of the lads to drive you to A & E. They can check you out for concussion as well. Meanwhile we'll catch 'The Nut' and lead him back." 'The Nut', so nick-named on the yard for obvious reasons, was grazing quietly but eyeing up the opposition.

"'Tis begging your pardon, boss, but I'd rather be getting back on, if that's all right with you. If I don't get straight back on there then 'tis he has won this particular round, and t'will be twice as hard the next time, so it will."

"To be perfectly honest, Terence, I doubt that there will be a next time. We've wasted a lot of time and energy on this horse. He isn't improving one jot. You could've been seriously injured today and that I am not prepared to put up with. Racing is hard enough as it is without adding a rogue horse into the mix. I'm afraid it's the end of the line for him!"

"'Tis such a shame, sir, begging your pardon," protested Tops. "Could we just not give him the one more chance? Sure there must be some way to get inside that disturbed mind that he has."

At that moment H chose to whinny a soft greeting and the vast chestnut slowly picked his way over towards him, arched his neck and they blew softly into each other's nostrils. The chestnut immediately flattened his ears and squealed.

"Watch him, sir!" hissed Tops. "This is where he whirls round and kicks the living daylights out of anything on four legs."

Tops made a grab for The Nut's reins but just as Stephen made to turn H away, he nickered softly again and the chestnut ears flicked back and forth uncertainly. He let out a huge sigh, as if all the weight of the world was on his shoulders, and stood nuzzling into H's mane.

"Well, I'll be damned!" exclaimed Stephen. "What do you make of that? It seems as if The Beast has made a friend."

"Bloody Hell! Well now, would y' believe that?" Tops was excited. "Boss, I think it's a terrible shame being out here on the gallops an' all and not giving this lad one last chance. Could we not just see if he'll go up along sides his new pal? To be sure we have nothing to lose."

Stephen was sceptical. "Well, we've already tried it with a dozen other horses to no avail. But as you say, we've nothing to lose, except perhaps my best stable jockey! Be it on your own head."

In a twinkling, before the boss could even think about changing his mind, Tops had vaulted into the saddle. He felt the horse stiffen and arch his back but Tops sat quietly, hardly daring to breathe. The boss turned towards the gallops, H stepping quietly onto the springy track. Nutcracker stood still as a statue, every joint stiff, every muscle tense as he watched H walk away from him. Tops dare not move in the saddle, he made no effort to pick up the reins for he could feel that one false move and this magnificent horse would be lost to them forever, lost in a world of hatred and fear.

Tops prayed silently as the distance became greater and greater.

"C'mon you great lump, can you not see that life is for living. 'Tis your last chance or t'will be the knackers for you."

"This isn't going to work, I'm afraid." Stephen reined in H. "You had better get off him and lead him home."

H turned his head and looked long and hard at the chestnut then with a squeal and a buck, which totally took his rider unawares, he set off at a flat-out gallop up the hill.

All this was just too much for Nutcracker who leapt forward and proceeded to eat up the ground until he caught up with the now slowing Humphrey. He overtook him in a bound and surged onwards in a long effortless stride. Tops had never sat on anything quite like it before. It was the nearest thing to flying he had ever experienced. He could feel the powerhouse underneath him. It was as if something in that huge body had broken free at last and the galloping was a gallop of exorcism and sheer joy. They thundered up the hill in a rush of wind and flying turf, horse and rider merging into one great flying machine. They galloped on and on, clearing the post and rail at the end of the gallops in an almighty leap and headed out into the open. Tops was powerless, so he sat and waited and steered as best he could to keep the flying hooves on the hard, narrow track beyond the rails. Eventually, Nutcracker slowed to a canter then a trot and finally to a walk and in a haze of steam and heaving flanks, a dazed Tops turned him for home. They met an anxious Stephen halfway along the track.

"My God, Terrence, are you all right? I really don't need any more excitement for today. The old ticker is going nineteen to the dozen. My God, that horse can gallop! What a horse! Are you both safe? I thought you were both going for the next county!"

Tops patted the dripping neck.

"He wasn't even trying, boss. I've a feeling, so I have, that this beast here has another gear yet to be showing us. Mind you, the old brakes need a bit of a refit surely so they do!" Tops peered through the dried blood on his face and grinned his cheeky grin. "'Tis the knackers for him then tomorrow, boss?" Stephen's stern features melted for a moment into a surprisingly sunny smile.

"No, my boy, it most certainly is not. With this old boy's help, we might just manage to get The Nut into training." He patted H affectionately and smiled secretly to himself as he passed the post and rails which, in the heat of the moment he and H had taken in their stride. "Mmm, there's some spark left in this old boy still," he said.

Tops looked at the double set of hoof prints under the post and rails and absolutely understood!

Chapter Eleven

The days turned into weeks and the great Rajah's Moon statue came out of the doldrums and stood proudly surrounded by a colourful riot of yellow daffodils and bright red tulips. The Nut's training began in earnest. He still had his bolshie moments but he and H were inseparable and as H's calming influence took effect, the Nuts' aggression seemed to somewhat abate. However, the grooms were still very wary of the flashing hooves and bared teeth. It was only Tops who was tolerated within the chestnut's personal space and the day to day care fell to him. As the horse became more trainable and much fitter his fast times on the gallops became a source of great excitement. His initial exuberant jumping even led to a sweepstake amongst the stable jockeys as to how many times Tops would be jumped off in the week! Fortunately, after a few weeks The Nut settled down properly into his work and as Tops didn't hit the ground any more the sweepstake was — much to Tops' relief — abandoned.

Throughout the months of training H was never far from the chestnut's side. Nuts would deign to go out of the yard and onto the gallops at first only with Tops on board and only if he was first of the string and following closely on H's tail. After a couple of months, one wondrous dawn, after a cavorting bronco busting session in the yard, he even allowed the stable race jockey, talented, wiry Mike Sands to school him over fences. Mike had been race jockey for Stephen for quite a few years. Experienced and talented as he was, even he found the raging chestnut a huge challenge.

"Bloody hell, boss!" he gasped. "I didn't know I had that much glue on my arse!"

"It's called self- preservation, lad! He'll be fine once he's out of the yard and following H." True to form, once on the gallops he cantered alongside his friend and then gradually eased away into his mind-blowing, ground-eating stride. After the numerous ejections of Tops over the schooling fences, he had settled to jump them with consummate ease, maintaining an easy rhythm and rarely making a mistake. Everything was going along famously — until the first race!

It was close to home, at Newbury. H travelled with Nuts in the three-and-a-half-ton horsebox. All went according to plan until the big chestnut had to leave his friend. Stephen and Tops managed, using all their skill and experience, to get Nuts to the paddock but he was wild and intractable. They managed to throw Mike up into the saddle as Nuts whirled round on the end of his lead rein but then all hell broke loose. The huge chestnut bucked and reared, spun round and refused to leave the paddock. All the efforts of Mike and Stephen and Tops were to no avail. As the others filed past him down to the start, the heaving chestnut completely lost the plot. Screaming constantly for his friend, adrenaline took over and the months and months of careful training flew straight out of the window!

It was a very silent despondent team who led the sweating, adrenalin-fuelled horse back to the horsebox.

The following morning it was grim faces round the office desk as they met to discuss the horse's future!

"This bloody effing horse!" was Stephen's opening cry. "What the bloody hell are we going to do with him? Such talent! Such psychological damage already done before we got him! Such a shame! I thought I was pretty knowledgeable about horses. Good at getting inside their oh, so, little brains, but this one, bloody hell he's humbling. If nothing else, he's taught me that I know nothing! It's very depressing to learn that the older you get the less you know! God, I wonder if he will ever do the job! At the moment all this work and effort we have put in seems to have got us absolutely nowhere! I feel we're coming to the end of the line here."

This was quite a long, passionate speech for the usually impassive Stephen, and Tops was quite taken aback.

"We can't give up now, boss, we just can't. All that work down the swanny and just look how far we've come. Just cast your mind back to his first few days here. He'll come around, so he will. Let's take him to some meetings where we can get Conker closer to the paddock and track. Let's go everywhere we can until he learns that his mate is always going to be there before and after each race."

"That's all very well, lad, but it's time, money and my reputation at stake here! No one wants to see their trainer having disasters at race meetings. It's not very good PR."

"With respect, boss, when have you ever been afraid of bad press?"

Stephen smiled a wry smile. "Never, lad, never. And you're right, I am not going to start now!

He grinned a rare grin, squared his shoulders and in a breath reinstated his positive, confident, some might say arrogant, self.

"OK, let's get a grip. Operation Team Nuts is a go and if it's not successful at least it won't be for want of trying! I'll enter him for Wetherby next week. What are you hanging round here for, Tops? Get those lads organised and let's get this show back on the road!"

Tops breathed a huge sigh of relief and gave the chestnut a severe talking to as he tacked him up for exercise. "'Tis a stupid bugger that y' are! Do y' not realise the talent you have? 'Tis surely time that you understood that we're all on your side. If you don't come right, me fine fellow, there'll be no one willing to kill themselves in Retrained Racehorse Classes so there won't. Indeed, 'twill be the bullet for you."

The big chestnut snaked his neck, showed the whites of his eyes and tried to take a chunk out of Tops' arm.

At Wetherby races the following week and after much discussion of options over Nut's stable door, they decided to try a different tack. Instead of bringing the dancing chestnut into the middle of the paddock to be mounted, Tops kept him moving forwards on the perimeter track next to the rails. A silent Mike was legged up on the move by a breathless Stephen. Mike, with his wealth of experience was very experienced and very talented and by now well used to the big chestnut and his intractable ways. But Tops could tell by his silence and by Stephen's terse expression that this was the most worrying moment for them all. How would the beast react?

"Please, please, horse, let's not be having a repeat of last week!" Tops whispered. His calming voice belied the frantic beating of his heart. An image shot into his mind of a swan, serene on top but paddling frantically in the water. That's just how he felt but knew this was not the time to transmit any trace of agitation down the leather lead rein to his restive charge for it was already taut enough. "There, there, me little man, 'tis fretting y'self y' are. Steady old chap, settle y'self down now." Whether these calm words made a difference or not, who knows? But Nuts, although shaking and sweating and occasionally blasting out a piercing whinny for his friend, did allowed Mike to settle in the plate. He then continued his springing dance around the paddock perimeter track.

"My God," hissed Stephen, "we may have cracked it. Follow that little bay horse, number seven, up to the racetrack and for God's sake keep the bugger moving."

Once released on the track everyone breathed a sigh of relief as the chestnut cantered up to the start on the little bay's heels. During the race, following orders, Mike kept him alongside the bay for as long as possible. Nuts jumped like a stag and pulled away over the last furlong to win by ten lengths. The long hard months of training had triumphed at last.

The next day, after a three years lapse, the big chestnut was once more in the racing press with the by-line, "Has the Nutcracker Cracked it at last?" Stephen smiled wryly as he read the paper over his morning coffee.

"Mm, we'll see," he mused, but there deep in his heart, beyond all the cynicism, nestled a tiny fragment of hope. He could feel it stirring.

The subsequent races became less and less traumatic for Team Nuts as long as certain rules were followed. Always H travelled as a calming influence to the mentally fragile Nutcracker. Always Tops was at the horse's head whispering nonsense in his soft Irish lilt. Always Mike was legged up on the run by a fitter Stephen, and always they found a bay horse to follow down to the start. If just one of these vital elements was missing then Nuts would revert back to his confused insecure self and would rear and plant his hooves and refuse to leave the paddock. After just one more disaster at Wetherby, when poor Tops had flu and was bedridden, Team Nuts really did crack it. They kept to the same routine and thanked their lucky stars that bay colouring was such a common gene.

Nearly a year to the day after Nuts' arrival Stephen announced the monumental news at the morning staff briefing that Nuts was entered in The Grand National. The greatest Steeplechase of all time. He had already run in six National Hunt races under Stephen's colours. He had won five in fine form and his resurrection from rogue to racing success was becoming great gossip amongst the racing fraternity. Claire Balding had waxed lyrical about him when he was a close second in the Welsh Grand National, a rare mistake at the last costing him the winner's trophy. His transformation seemed nothing short of miraculous.

Throughout all the months of training H remained a steadying influence. He led the dawn string onto the gallops always with Nutcracker closely tucked in behind. Stephen usually in the saddle or if short of time and watching from his Range Rover, then H was ridden by one of the stable jockeys. He was a firm favourite with all the stable lads and young Johnny came over most weekends to ride him and have lunch with Stephen. Jim or Jane Collins would drop him off or pick him up and gradually the barrier between the two brothers was slowly dismantled. The Collins family invited Stephen often for Sunday lunch and they began to accompany him to race meetings. Johnny always rode with his hero, Tops, in the horsebox and was given the responsibility of looking after Conker, the invaluable companion.

Finally, the great day dawned. Well, actually dawn had not yet broken when in the cold four a.m. blackness, Tops struggled in the horizontal sleet to feed his charges. He was greeted by a nicker of welcome from the honest bay's striped face and by a squeal of anger from the bad tempered star of the show. The big chestnut showing his displeasure at being disturbed so early by sinking his teeth into Tops' forearm as he tipped the feed into the manger.

"Ouch! You bloody great shit! That hurt!" Tops rubbed his arm ruefully and thanked his lucky stars that he was wearing his warm padded jacket! "And the top o' the morning t' you too you miserable git! If you weren't so difficult, we could've stabled at Aintree overnight, so we could. 'Twould be grand, so it would, if y' could just be slightly on the generous side today and make your way up to the start without too much trouble." The big chestnut rolled his eyes and kicked out as Tops made for the door "Well! No change there then. I guess it's just another day for you. Now then, my bonny lad." Tops moved next door and the bay snuffled into Tops' thatch of hair, the warm breath twisting mist into the cold air.

"If only the horror next door had just a tiny piece of your lovely patient temperament. Could y' just have quiet word and tell him that he has to behave today for to be sure, the whole universe will be watching!" Tops absently stroked the gleaming neck and felt that lovely sense of peace that flows so often in the harmonious energy between man and beast. His quiet moment of reverie was rudely broken by Stephen's booming tones.

"Tops — what on earth are you doing? Are these horses fed yet? Come along, lad, let's get a move on. We have to leave at five!"

"Right, boss, just feeding. Don't worry, we'll be on the road by five. Bloody hell!" he muttered to H under his breath. "You and I will have to have the patience of saints today, so we will, for to be sure the boss and The Nut will be just as stressed and difficult as each other!"

True to his word, by five the horsebox was turning out of the yard gates, the headlights turning the striations of the bark of the great redwood trunks into a myriad of patterns. Johnny, as always, was accompanying Tops in the horsebox and Stephen, Jim and Jane were coming along later in the Jag.

Aintree, when they arrived just before nine, was a cauldron of energy. A bubbling expectancy waiting to erupt. The roads toward the racecourse were busy and congested as excited race goers made their way towards the greatest jump race in their calendar.

H came off the waggon with his usual measured step, carefully placing each hoof delicately on the ramp and looking around him with ears pricked in interest.

Conversely the great chestnut, as usual, flew off the ramp from top to bottom in one gargantuan leap and fly-bucked all the way to the stable. Tops, gritting his teeth, muttered profanities under his breath and hung on for grim death.

"Tops! Do you want me to help?" Johnny volunteered, leading a placid H on the end of a looping lead rope.

"No, I fecking don't! No offence, son, but just stay out of the fecking way and get H to go in front." Johnny was quite taken aback. He had never heard Tops swear before and with great perspicacity for one so young, realised that nerves on this momentous occasion were even getting to his hero. He battened down his excitement muttered a meek, "OK" and hustled H into the front.

Stephen and the Collins' arrived later in the morning.

"How is he lad?"

"Looking fine, boss. A bit stressy but that's par for the course."

"Humph!" Stephen looked at the sweating chestnut walking his box like the wall of death, and wasn't convinced.

"Why not bring Conker out and stand him up close to the box door? Maybe that'll settle him."

H was duly led out and the big chestnut and the little bay blew a greeting into each other's nostrils. Nuts squealed, gave H a nip then stood quietly with his muzzle resting on his neck. “Wow, look at that! Awesome! It’s magic!” Johnny danced in delight on the end of H’s lead rope.

Stephen breathed a sigh of relief. “My God! I race horses nearly every day of the week. Why am I so nervous about this one?”

Jane gave her brother-in-law’s arm a squeeze. “Perhaps because this is the most famous steeplechase in the world and because you have brought a horse here which was on the brink of being put down a few months ago! The fact that he’s here at all is such a tribute to your training. Everything else that happens today is just a bonus.”

Stephen gave her one of his rare twinkling smiles that actually reached and softened his steel-grey eyes. “You are so right, my dear. I and the team have actually got him this far — the rest is up to him! If we can get him down to the start we’ll be laughing!”

The rest of the day seemed to pass very slowly. Lunch was booked in the Owner’s and Trainer’s restaurant, but no one wanted to eat much, and conversation was minimal. They took it in turns to lead H to stand outside the restless chestnut’s stable. Finally, the big race loomed closer.

“Right everyone!” commanded Stephen, “Thirty minutes to go before he’s due in the paddock. Let’s get him to the saddling area. Come on, all hands to the wheel.” Stephen immediately switched into his professional mode and everyone jumped to it. Johnny put H back in his stable and the recalcitrant chestnut was led to the saddling up box. He fidgeted and whinnied for his companion and flashed out with his hind legs in annoyance when the girth was tightened. Tops swore under his breath as the snaking head thumped into his cheek but eventually he was tacked up to Stephen's satisfaction.

"OK, everyone, this is it! Hopefully we'll see you in the paddock. Let's keep everything as calm as possible and not deviate from our normal routine. This is just another race to Nuts. Thank God he doesn't know it's the Grand National!" A memory flew into Stephen's mind of a TV interview with one of the Olympic event riders who had had a disastrous cross-country round "Unfortunately my horse didn't know he was at The Olympics!" he had said wryly. The memory gave Stephen some comfort and he smiled. "Blooming horses! Now Tops, hang fire until you see that bay horse leave. The one that's being girthed up three boxes down and then nip in smartly behind him and I'll bring up the rear."

"Oh bejesus!" muttered Tops as he saw the bay leave the saddling box. "Tis worse than army manoeuvres so it is! Come on you great oaf. Now! Quick march!" Nuts spied the bay in front of him and danced and pranced beside Tops, nearly pulling him off his feet, trying to catch up. Stephen hurried along behind, all thoughts of being cool and calm deserting him as he tried to juggle his binoculars, flapping tie and his race card whilst on the run.

In this ungainly fashion the hasty trio finally made it to the paddock. The race goers hanging on the rails breathed a big sigh of relief and a hopeful few rushed to put on their last minute bets. If the unpredictable chestnut had made it this far then maybe he stood a chance of making it to the start! Nuts, a few metres behind the bay, had settled into his huge purposeful walk. Tops was on the point of jogging to keep up with the giant strides. Snatches of conversation floated past him.

"Wow! That's that difficult chestnut, The Nutter!"

"D'you think he stands a chance?"

"No way! They'll never get him to the start."

"I'm not backing that! It's high odds, 20 to 1, but it'll never start."

Tops kept marching and tried not to think of the £400 he'd scraped together to back his charge. "I know you can do it if only you try, for to be sure, you have all the talent in the world. Don't you be letting us all down today, me lad!"

Nuts looked neither right nor left but strode onward with his ears locked on the bay rump a few metres ahead.

The jockeys came into the paddock and each horse was led to the centre and surrounded by his own little group of excited owners and terse trainers. Not so Nutcracker, he just kept striding along the perimeter track with a breathless Stephen and Mike running alongside. With split second timing, Stephen threw his jockey up into the plate. Nutcracker pinned his ears back but never broke stride. Mike settled his feather weight and patted the sweating neck.

"Any last-minute instructions, boss?"

"No lad, it's in the lap of the God's now! Just keep him moving then follow the bay up to the start and keep him close. Good luck!"

Stephen's response was cheerful but his heart was in his mouth and his face ashen. Nutcracker chose that moment to stop dead. He reared up vertically, teetering for a moment on the knife edge of balance. There was an audible sigh from the punters on the rails and the brave few who'd backed him looked sadly at their betting slips. Mike threw his weight forward, clutching the muscled neck. For a moment it seemed as if horse and jockey were on the brink of the precipice of disaster. Then the fates chose to smile and gravity prevailed to bring the pair back down. Tops managed to avoid the twirling forelegs and reorganised himself at the horse's head.

"Not now, horse," he pleaded. "Oh bejesus, not now."

The chestnut reared again, catching Tops' shoulder as he came down.

"Ouch, y' bugger." Beside himself with pain and embarrassment, Tops elbowed the horse in the shoulder and the enraged chestnut planted his hooves, refused to move and sank his teeth into Tops' arm. "Double ouch, ye fecking thing!"

"Don't fret lads!" a cheery voice rang out. "Just tuck in behind me." It was Chris Young, Champion jockey and long-time friend of Mike's, riding the favourite Maestroman. Nuts watched the big bay gelding stride past him and then ears pricked and with all the placidity of a little lamb, followed sweetly in his wake.

Stephen, in a maelstrom of emotion and with a sinking heart, watched them go out of the paddock towards the track.

"I'm going to have a coronary before this bloody horse ever gets to the start."

"No you're not." Jane put a comforting arm around him. "The worst is over. C'mon, let's go into the Owners' and Trainers' stand to watch."

Tops, without any further ado, led Nuts to the track to parade in front of the grandstand and then unclipped the lead rein. The big chestnut launched himself into the air and then listening to Mike's light hand on the rein and with the bay favourite alongside, he settled into a steady canter as they went down to look at the first fence.

Tops breathed a huge sigh of relief and made his way to the rails at the finishing post. On the way he prayed fervently to a God he'd never much acknowledged before.

"Please, please, please, let the bugger at least start!"

The Collins' all made their way to the stands in tense silence.

The race passed in a blur. Stephen, stony-faced behind his binoculars, Jim inscrutable. Jane with her head in her hands. Only Johnny was beside himself with excitement and gave a running commentary.

"He's started — awesome! The Nut has started! Mum, Dad, Uncle Stephen, he's running!

"He's in the middle of the field! He's over the first and the second. Oh my God, he nearly fell at the chair but the commentator says he's OK. He's coming to Becher's. He's not been mentioned for ages! He must've fallen at Becher's! No! No, they say he's over Becher's! He's completed the first circuit. Oh look, I can see him on the big screen, he's still in the middle. Oh, come on, Nut, do your thing. He's coming through to the outside. He's lying sixth! The guy on the loudspeaker has just said he's jumping like a machine and he's full of running. Uncle Stephen, he's a machine and he's full of running!" Johnny tugged at Stephen's sleeve. "Uncle Stephen, Uncle Stephen, are you listening!" Johnny started to jump up and down in excitement and continued with his own breathless commentary. "He flew the last. He's third in the final straight. He's losing ground. He's gaining ground! It's neck and neck. It's awesome! It's a photo! Mum, Uncle Stephen, it's a photo finish!"

Time stood still! Stephen, Jim and Jane hardly dared to breathe. Tops on the finishing rail, listening to the commentary over the loudspeakers, felt the earth beneath his feet tremble as the horses flashed past him in a blur of colour and sound. He thought he saw Nutcracker up there but he couldn't be sure. His brain didn't seem to be functioning properly. He only knew he had to move fast to get to the horse's head and lead him back in to the paddock.

The loudspeakers bellowed "The winner of the Grand National is number six, Nutcracker." The whole stadium erupted in a roar of approval. "Second, number twelve Maestroman, third…

Stephen didn't hear anymore because the whole world around him seemed to have shut down into a slow motion silent film.

Jane and Johnny were shrieking in his ears! "He won! He won! He won! C'mon, let's get down to the winner's enclosure!"

"My God, I can't believe it!" A bemused Stephen was led down through a throng of well-wishers to the enclosure.

Chris Young, riding alongside Mike back towards the stands, leaned over and gave him a hefty thwack on the back! "Should've left you in the paddock, you sod! Won't be so kind next time! Well done, mate!" he grinned. "You and your lot have so deserved this! I'll get you next time!"

"Next time — don't be daft!" Laughed Mike.

Tops, grinning like a Cheshire cat waited to lead the chestnut giant, flanked by two police horses, down the walkway. The crowd was fifteen deep leaning over the rails all trying to shake Mike's hand and pat the sweating chestnut neck. Nuts strode purposefully, his heaving flanks settling into a less erratic rhythm as he walked, and true to form, he couldn't resist snaking his neck and tried to take a chunk out of the neck of one of his escorts.

"Watch him," Tops called "He's a bit of a bugger, this one, so he is! He's no respecter of persons — not even the police!" The crowd roared with delight. Loving the fact that this untrainable underdog of a horse had just pulled off the biggest jump race in the calendar and was still as feisty as ever.

He stood in the winner's enclosure and whinnied frantically for his stable companion.

The indomitable, enthusiastic Clare Balding thrust her microphone under Stephen's nose.

"Here is Stephen Collins. The owner and trainer of the winning horse, Nutcracker. What a special moment this is for you and your team. How do you feel, Mr Collins?"

Stephen, aware that most of the world was watching and listening, tried to pull himself together. "This is a wonderful moment. I always had a feeling that this horse was very special and it's a great tribute to all my team that he's won this race and the glory has to go to all of them."

"I understand that this horse has not been easy to train?"

"No!" Stephen replied wryly. "You could say that — never easy! There was a time when we thought his career as a racehorse was over. In fact, a time when he was literally good for nothing and a danger to have around. That's when we… well we…" His words trailed off as the full magnitude of this glorious success flew unbidden to his heart and he turned away from the camera. "Excuse me a moment. I think I have something in my eye."

"In fact," Jane came swiftly to the rescue, "we seriously considered having him put down. He was just so dangerous and no one could ride him." She then completely sabotaged her rescue attempt by promptly busting into floods of tears. "Sorry," she sobbed "So sorry."

Little Johnny chipped in. "Conker saved him. My uncle's hack. He's a fab horse and I ride him and everything and he saved Nuts because he liked him and he followed him that day onto the gallops and it was his last chance to come good!"

Clare Balding was fascinated and knew this was good TV. She expertly dodged the snaking chestnut neck and concentrated her attention on the young boy.

"I've heard that Nutcracker had a companion who travels to all the race meetings. Is he here now?"

"Yes, there he is!" H was standing by the walkway to the stables and the cameras panned over to him.

"It's the bright bay horse over there!" Tops prompted. "He's the reason we managed to train this horse. To be sure, a year ago we couldn't even get the bugger, oops sorry, the blighter, out of the stable yard. He was worthless, so he was and now... and now." Tops swallowed hard and for the first time ever in his life ran out of words.

"And now," continued Clare, taking over in her friendly professional way, "This magnificent difficult horse has just won the Grand National — the greatest steeplechase in the world. No wonder emotions here are running high." The camera panned to the giant head-tossing chestnut and then to a close up of his owner and trainer. There, in front of millions of viewers world-wide, was the normally impassive Stephen Collins patting the chestnut neck with tears streaming down his cheeks.

Nutcracker, becoming even more impatient, whinnied frantically for his companion and began to fly buck in the winner's enclosure, scattering cameramen and the press journalists in all directions. H whinnied back from the stable walkway. Nutcracker raised his head and pricked his ears in the direction of the stables. One lucky photographer, avoiding the mayhem, managed to capture this one instant — Nutcracker standing like a rock, a great golden statue of a horse. This was the picture that graced the front of the Racing Post and the tabloids the following day. His second time around amazing leap over Becher's was on the front cover of Horse and Hound the following week and caused even the most cynical of its readers to gasp in awe.

Chapter Twelve

The Lawson family were clustered round the TV on Grand National day, glued to the build-up and the race. The twins, forgetting that they were soon to be cool teenagers of thirteen, had been shrieking with excitement as the two horses battled neck and neck for the finishing post.

"Oh my God, what an awesome horse!"

"Don't blaspheme, dear."

"Oh Mother, for God's sake!"

Annabel Lawson shrugged her shoulders and gave up.

"He is certainly the most beautiful horse and what a race he's won. That was such a thrilling finish. Oh look, that's his companion horse who has to go to every race meeting. Oh my God, it looks just like Humphrey!"

"Don't blaspheme, Mum!" was Sam's tart rejoinder. "But you're absolutely right, it's a dead ringer for H."

"Poor H, I wonder what happened to him? I still miss him even now. He was such a star."

The phone rang in the hall but no one could drag themselves away from the TV or the ensuing discussion.

"Rewind to the bit where they show the companion. I'm sure it was Humphrey." Annabel grabbed the remote. "It's him look!"

"It can't be." Charlie was unconvinced.

"It is!"

"It isn't!"

"Will someone get that damn phone!" George Lawson was losing patience. "Annabel, it's bound to be for you."

"You're right. It's probably Mrs Turner wittering on about the Church fete again."

Annabel dragged herself away from the reruns and made her way into the hall. Wafts of conversation came through to the lounge.

"Major Bentley, what a lovely surprise. How are you? Oh good! What? That's exactly what we thought. We're looking at the reruns and trying to decide. The girls are absolutely convinced."

"Hey everyone, guess what." she called through to the lounge. "Major B has just been watching the National. He's convinced the companion horse is Humphrey."

"Told you! Told you!" the twins screamed in unison "Quick, get off the phone. Mum, let's ring round everyone and see what they think and then we can ring the trainer, what's-his-face, and find out more."

Whilst the Lawsons were busy on their phones, Matt the Australian vet and Charlene, Jack Flash's very ex, were actually at the Aintree meeting and were at that very moment studying the bay companion as he was waiting to be loaded for home. They had explained to Tops that after seeing the horse flashed up for an instant on the big screen they just had to come and see for themselves. Tops was fascinated as Matt went over all the scars and explained how they had arisen and how he had treated the injured horse after the dreadful night of the party at Flashlands. In mid-discussion, Charlene's mobile rang.

"Now then, darlin'." Charlene's face went ashen as she recognised the famous cockney drawl.

"Oh shit, it's him. Matt, it's him!" she whispered "How did he ever get my new number?" Matt leaned over and pressed loudspeaker.

"Darlin', I've just watched the big race and I'm going to buy the winner and have that other little horse, what's-its-name, back to ride. Thought you might like to come back with him so we can ride together." There were lots of loud guffaws in the background from Jack's obnoxious mates who were busy partying and being sycophantic as usual.

"Over my dead body!" Charlene retorted.

"And mine!" chipped in Matt and Tops in unison.

"You!" said Charlene vehemently, gaining confidence from Matt and Tops' verbal support and from Matt's protective arm around her shoulders, "You are the most despicable person I have ever met. Go back to your drugs and molls and alcohol and never ever phone me again."

"Well done, my little Sheila," Matt squeezed her hand and shouted into the speaker.

"And that goes for me too, you pretentious little shit!"

Jack, barely comprehending any of this in his addled state, slurred a "Bye then, darlin'." and turned back to his mates and to his grand piano and to the beautiful blonde draped over the keys.

"No worries!" grinned Matt. "Not worth a sheep's arse! C'mon girl, let's all go have a drink!"

Across the country in North Yorkshire, Jade and Gareth had been out for a spin that Saturday on Gareth's new Harley and heard nothing until the next morning. The phone rang early. Gareth stretched lazily for the phone and gazed down at the sleeping Jade beside him. Still in awe of her natural yet sultry beauty, he studied her as she lay sweetly as a baby. Her face peaceful, her only piercings now a tiny stud in her navel and a set of three descending small hoops in her ear. Their unlikely relationship was flourishing and although often stormy, they were learning a great deal from each other as they walked together along their undulating path. Jade was finally beginning to trust this 'posh bloke' as she described him to her friends. She had even been persuaded into a slinky silver dress for the hunt ball and had wowed everyone with her amazing figure, dark beauty and earthy conversation. Gareth was learning to be less arrogant and less selfish as he grew more and more enamoured by this unusual, interesting girl. The bottom line was that rather like Henry Higgins and Eliza, they moved from disdain to hesitating attraction to deep affection and possible love. At first only daring to dart briefly into each other's worlds, they eventually became so happy and confident with each other that these worlds went from collision course to an interwoven orbit of mainly peace.

“Yes, uncle!” Gareth sat up quickly, startling Jade awake. “Oh what? I don’t believe it. How bloody marvellous.”

“What? What? WHAT?” Jade pinched his arm.

“Ouch that hurt. No nothing, uncle it’s fine. Sh sh,” he hissed at Jade. “It’s the Major. He thinks they’ve seen H. Yes, yes, of course, that’s wonderful news. I’ll have a look on the internet and get back to you.”

He turned excitedly to Jade. “They think they’ve seen H on TV at the National meeting. The horse that won has a companion and everyone thinks it could be H.”

“Wow!” Jade was out of bed in a flash running to get the iPad. Ever impatient, she was beside herself whilst she waited for it to connect. “C’mon you stupid bloody thing hurry up!”

“Be quiet woman, it’s going as fast as it can!” Finally, Google found the big race and the photos.

“There, oh look! It’s him! Oh my God, it is him!” Jade threw her arms around Gareth’s neck and promptly burst into tears.

Texts and emails flew around the county and beyond, so that on the Sunday, a week later when Stephen had a party at Redwoods to celebrate his momentous win, a host of people were gathered around Nutcracker’s box. He eyed them suspiciously, laid his ears back and munched on his haylage. Stephen, taking no chances and not wishing to be sued for some horrible injury, had wisely put up a grill to protect Nuts’ adoring fans. Around the box next door, however, was also a great throng of people quaffing champagne and making enough noise to out-decibel The Thornbury Brass Band.

Stephen, Tops and the Lawson family listened in amazement as H's chequered life unfolded from the different conversations.

"Oh my God," Jade was exclaiming, resting drunkenly against Gareth's protective frame. "I love this horse. I looked after him years ago when he was Major B's hunter."

"And a bloody good hunter he was too." Major B and Lavinia had made a weekend of it and each on their fourth glass of champers were on sparkling form. "Unfortunately, my wild, at the time nephew, nearly killed him! Twice in fact!" Gareth had the candour to look rather shame-faced but then Jade planted a huge drunken kiss on his lips and slurred, "But he's lovely now because he has me and I'm such a steadying influence and I lurve him." Everyone erupted in laughter.

"What? What've I said?"

"And," chipped in Charlie, "he helped me save Mum's life. He made me get on H and jump him over his huge motorbike when he broke his leg and nearly killed my mother in the woods."

"Hang on. You make me sound like some sort of axe murderer!"

"And," chipped in Sam, not to be outdone by her twin. "He was stolen from Thornbury show, not Gareth, H, and we were all heartbroken. I thought I would die I cried so much."

"Can you believe it?" Stephen managed to get a word in. "I even went to see him in Ireland and then went to buy him at the sale but he'd already gone."

"I treated him," said Matt. "When Jack Flash owned him."

"Ohmygod" the twins gasped. "Not *the* Jack Flash, we just love that album, Crazy Mermaid, and his latest, 'Cyber Stream'. He is just awesome."

"Not so awesome if you knew him like I do!" piped up Charlene, she just couldn't help herself. "He's a horrible person. I should know, I went out with him for long enough."

"OH. MY. GOD! You went out with the great Jack Flash. Oh, how super cool is that!" The twins were awestruck.

"What's more," said Mrs Beans. "I was his housekeeper for many years and if it hadn't been for Charlene and Matt here this lovely horse would've died."

"Tell us more about Jack Flash," the twins insisted but by the time Matt and Charlene had finished their stories they looked very crestfallen. They couldn't quite believe that their hero was just not the person they imagined him to be.

"Right, that's it! I am going to bin Crazy Mermaid and never listen to his music again," declared Charlie. "How could he treat poor old H like that?" She kissed his soft muzzle in sympathy.

"What a prick!" said Sam.

"Sammy, enough!" her father scolded. "We're all thinking it but trust you to say it!"

Old John grinned and gave H a pat and another of his prize carrots. "Now then, old lad, don't like 'osses much mysel but you was always a bit special." H blew into the wrinkled old hand and delicately took the tasty offering.

Bit by bit, H's amazing story was pieced together and the colourful jigsaw of his life slowly grew bigger and bigger. There were many interjections and oohs and aahs, particularly during the Jack Flash episodes and the dreadful days when H nearly died after his days on the beach. Johnny was in full flow, explaining to his rapt audience how they put H into the sling when a vision in pink appeared at his side. Felicity! Still a stately galleon, with pink sails billowing, she parted the sea of people.

"Wow, Felicity, how awesome to see you again." Johnny flung his arms around her and gave her a big bear hug. "This is Felicity! He explained to everyone "She's a horse witch. She whispered a spell into H's ear and saved him."

Felicity giggled. "Less of the witch, young Johnny, and more of the whisperer if you don't mind."

There were jovial introductions all round and then, after a few more whispers with H, Felicity shocked everyone by moving towards Nutcracker's box. In one swift movement and before anyone could react, she had unbolted the door and was inside.

"Bloody hell," shouted Stephen "What are you doing woman? Don't go in there! You'll get hurt!"

Fed up with all the noise and clamour disturbing his haylage time, Nuts lunged at her, ears flat. Felicity spoke some soft incomprehensible words that no one could fathom and stood her ground. Nuts sank his teeth into a flowing pink sleeve, the cloth ripped and his teeth drew blood on Felicity's fleshy arm. Everyone gasped and Stephen lunged for the door.

"Don't anyone move!" Felicity hissed as she continued a whispered stream of unintelligible words.

Nuts, ears still flattened, snaked his head for another strike. Felicity gently raised her hand in a stop gesture, her diamond rings twinkling. Amidst the stream of whispered phrases Nuts snaked his neck threateningly but the lunging bite never came. He eyed her suspiciously but his ears were no longer pinned to his head but flicked back and forth in question. Felicity continued the stream of hushed words and Nutcracker stood quietly and listened. He then stretched out his glossy chestnut neck and allowed her to place her chubby ringed fingers on his forehead. The silence was tangible. No one hardly dared to breathe. The big chestnut let out a huge sigh and blew softly into Felicity's arm.

"My Gawd," whispered Stephen "I've never seen anything like it. How is she doing that?"

Not for the first time did Stephen realise that there were things going on in the energy flow between man and beast that were way beyond his understanding. Here was a huge pink froth of a woman mesmerising a damaged horse with inane whispering. The mind boggled.

Across the yard one of the lads dropped a bucket with a loud clang. The Nut whirled away and the spell was broken.

"Well, my dear." Stephen rebolted the door. "In all my life with horses I have never quite seen anything like that before. Perhaps you'd like to come down here before Nuts' races and give him some mental therapy."

Felicity looked for the derision in the steel-grey eyes, but found only a soft appreciative gleam.

"Why not? I would love to help him. He is not beyond comforting and the grey horse over there, box walking, I'll go and have a word with him too. If I may."

Stephen nodded, feeling quite overpowered himself by this strange woman. He shook his head to clear his thoughts and at that moment Johnny dashed up and grabbed his arm.

"Uncle Stephen. Isn't this just awesome? Conker's really called Humphrey or 'H'. What shall we call him now?"

"I don't know, lad." Stephen ruffled his nephew's hair. "You choose."

"I'm going to ask Tops what he thinks. You know what? I love this place and I love you too, Uncle Stephen." With that, he ran off to speak to Tops. Stephen felt a lump rise in his throat as he looked around at his yard, his horses, his family and his new-found noisy friends. They were still clustered around the two loose boxes quaffing champagne, their excitement and laughter ringing through the clear spring air. The object of their cacophony, the peaceful but scarred bright bay horse with a crooked white stripe, he munched steadily on his carrots and said not a word.